PickLEWITCH and Jack

CLAIRE BARKER

Illustrated by Teemu Juhani

FABER & FABER

Prologue:

The Dreadful Strangers

A fierce gale had been slashing at the shrubbery since lunchtime, pouncing on the weathervane and snorting wetly through the keyholes. CRASH and SMASH went the plant pots. CREAK and CLANG went the rusty gates. It was a five-star hullabaloo that shook the old place to its roots.

'What lovely weather we're having!' cried the strange little girl, perched high in the branches of the old walnut tree. 'Wheeee!' she squealed, holding on to her pointed hat as the tree pitched back and forth like a fairground ride. Her dungarees were bejewelled in birds and her hair was as red as a robin's breast. 'FASTER!' she laughed. 'MORE!'

On command a blizzard of copper leaves rose up from the ground, swirling and merging into one giant, beastly shadow that loomed over the tree. It reared up on to its back legs and let out a blood-curdling howl that rattled the roof tiles for miles around.

'A storm wolf!' gasped the girl, gazing upwards in admiration. 'Oh whizz-cracking!' she applauded 'Bravo!'

The beast bowed graciously, dived back down to the ground and kicked the bins over with a BANG. He was about to show off a bit more, when his ears pricked up at the growl of an engine and the crunch of tyres on gravel. The storm wolf instantly dropped to a shy breeze and slunk behind the potting shed.

The girl swung around. She sniffed sharply at the cool air and a blast of birds exploded into the sky, filling the air with harsh cries. 'Who goes there?' she muttered, fumbling for her binoculars. 'Who be you, so rudely interrupting? Friend or foe?'

A piano, beds and chairs poured like a trail of ants out of the big yellow removal lorry, straight into the house. 'Boxies ahoy,' she scowled, shrugging a starling off her shoulder. 'Fudgenuts and bats' bums.'

Down on the ground, a boy slipped out of the passenger seat of the lorry. Intrigued, the girl polished her lenses and zoomed in for a closer look.

The boy seemed to be about the same age as her

and around the same height, but any similarity ended there. She studied his clean shoes and buttoned-up cardigan, noting with interest the shiny smoothness of his hair. She touched her own hair: it was very different, full of fluff and twigs. Sometimes the cheeky sparrows got in and she had to bang her head with a stick to make them leave.

'What a peculiar person,' she said in prim tones. 'Most curious and odd. And such bad manners too, arriving without an invitation.' Her tummy let out a long rumble and she straightened her hat. 'I hope he's brought cake.'

1

Peek-a-Woo

Rookery Heights, having been empty for years, was cold and smelled of damp. It was creepy, full of creaks and squeaks and secretive corners. The half-unpacked boxes made cruel angles in the twilight and clothes hung from a rail like ghosts.

Tucked up in a ball inside his sleeping bag, Jack lay with his eyes were wide open and the hairs tingled on the back of his neck. He had a weird sense of being watched, a feeling he hadn't been able to shake since the moment they had arrived.

To make matters worse, the wind had picked up again and was prowling around the house, scrambling across the roof and thumping at the doors. He could hear the trees wooshing and wailing in the garden below so he covered his ears to block it out.

When his mum had told him they had inherited an old house with a bit of land, Jack had hoped this meant a spacious lawn for kicking a football about and a few apple trees to climb. He'd crossed his fingers that there would be a greenhouse, maybe a rope-swing or even room for a trampoline.

But instead it turned out to be like something from an eerie fairytale. The garden was surrounded by a high wall, crumbling and draped in thick cobwebs and a dark, damp stain seeping up through the brickwork. Barbed-wire brambles whipped and looped over the top as if to say 'KEEP OUT' and the only entrance – a rickety blue door – was barricaded shut with thick ropes of ivy, ferns squeezing through its rusty hinges. Above it rooks and crows patrolled the sky like sentries, screeching their ragged, off-key warnings. It was unwelcoming, strange and dangerous, and Jack didn't like it one bit.

Peeking through the small gap in the zip, Jack could see spindly tree shadows projected on to the window. *They look just like old men's arms*, he thought, *reaching out to grab me* ... In a panic he sprang out of bed, shut the curtains tightly and leapt straight back into his sleeping bag, his heart pounding.

Back in bed, he tried to slow his breathing. *Don't be silly, Jack; nobody's watching you. Think about it: trees don't have arms; so they can't reach things. A tree is a tree, plain and simple. Those are just shadows. There's nothing to worry about.*

Winner of 'Most Sensible Boy' for three years running at his last school, Jack wasn't normally one to be ruled by an overactive imagination. He knew very well that there was a perfectly logical explanation for everything if only you were prepared to look. Jack breathed deeply, closed his eyes tight and whispered times tables until his heart stopped banging. '*Ten times twenty-four is two hundred and forty, eleven times twenty-four is two hundred and sixty-four, twelve times twenty-four is two hundred and eighty-eight.*'

Eventually he was able to open one eye. The scary moonshadows had gone and he felt very relieved. *The wind isn't even howling really,* he thought, listening carefully. *It's more of a 'WOOOO' which is nowhere near as scary. Owls go WOOO and owls are simply part of the natural world. Owls, not howls.* He managed a smiled for the first time since he had arrived.

Feeling bolder, Jack decided to go a step further. *I want to see the stars but I can't with the curtains shut. Who knows?* he thought, wriggling out of his sleeping bag and padding across the squeaky floorboards, *maybe one day I might become an astronaut and then I'll need to know everything about the night sky.* He seized the curtains and whipped them back with a flourish.

A grubby little face stared straight back at him through the glass. 'WOOOO,' it shouted, 'WOOOOOOO!'

Jack shrieked and raced out of his room, screaming like a kettle: 'MUUM-MUUUM-MUM!'

'Jack?' His mum dashed up the stairs. 'Jack, are you all right? *Whatever* is the matter?'

'There's a girl!' he wailed, pointing back towards the bedroom. 'She's outside the window, looking in! She's ... wearing ... a hat!'

'A hat? What sort of hat? A girl? What?' Jack's mum strode down the corridor, into his bedroom and switched on the light.

'A ... a pointy one,' Jack said, hiding behind her.

Jack's mum peered out into the darkness. 'There's nothing there, Jack. Look for yourself.'

Jack edged towards the window. 'But she was definitely there,' he pleaded. 'Cross my heart and

13

hope to die. She was going "woooo" like that.'

'Oh, Jack,' sighed his mum. 'It's just the bad weather tonight. How on earth could a little girl get all the way up to an attic window? And in the dark too? This isn't like you at all – you're usually so *sensible*.' She raised an eyebrow. 'What's our motto? "Facts not fiction", remember?'

'*But, Mum, she was real,*' whispered Jack, peering out into the darkness of the garden, his breath white on the cold glass.

His mum closed the curtains again and tucked him back into his sleeping bag. 'It must have been your reflection, Jack. It's the only logical explanation. Now, try to get a good night's sleep. You've got a big day ahead of you tomorrow.' She paused for a moment and sat down on the edge of his bed, squeezing his hand. 'I really want you to be happy here, Jack,' she said softly. 'You deserve a good friend. I know things haven't been easy lately but this can be a new beginning for both of us: my new job at the surgery and you with your scholarship. Everything will be better now, I promise.' She stood up and smiled. 'I know, I'll make you some cakes to take in tomorrow to share – how about that? Everybody likes cakes! Let's start as we mean to go on, eh?' She kissed him on the forehead. 'Just don't wear yourself out before it's begun.'

She turned off the light and left, gently pulling the door closed behind her. Jack wriggled right down into the bottom of his sleeping bag, turned his back firmly to the window and squeezed his eyes tight shut. It was quiet. There were no more 'wooo's'. He counted his heartbeats in Spanish and then Russian and then Mandarin. He eventually drifted off into a fitful slumber, full of nightmares about prowling wolves and tangly, brambly, fairytale woods.

Luckily for him he missed the sound of something landing heavily in the shrubbery below the window, because that wouldn't have helped his anxiety one little bit.

2

Robber Burd

Jack left for school in an optimistic mood, swinging the bag of cakes, still warm from the oven. He was wide awake in spite of the strange events of the night before. 'Bad dreams are only to be expected,' he said to himself as he walked briskly down the street. 'Nothing to worry about! Just the first night in a new house.' Jack had an exciting day ahead: a new middle school, a new teacher and, very importantly, a chance to make new friends. It was the start of a thrilling adventure and nothing was going to spoil it.

Jack was a star performer in the classroom. Brilliant at maths, super at science and excellent at English, he was all-round-clever head-boy material. At his last school the other children had given him a nickname: Little Lord Smartypants. When it was announced that he'd won a scholarship to St Immaculate's School for the Gifted his classmates had been so happy they'd cheered, unlike his teacher who had sobbed.

Jack marched along, whistling in the sunshine, talking to himself out loud and making plans for his future. 'I'm going to shine as an academic star.' He smiled at the golden lion crest on his blazer pocket with pride. 'I'll be the best turned-out boy in the school. I'll share my cakes and make lots of new clever friends. No one will push me in puddles or call me names ever again.'

What he *didn't* see coming was the massive

pigeon poo that fell out of the sky – SPLAT – right on to his new blazer, covering the crest like a hideous badge. Jack looked down in horror as a one-legged bird swerved under his arm, swiped his bag of cakes and flapped off into the distance. 'OI!' he shouted, running after it. 'Thief! Give that back right now!'

The pigeon got off to a good start but it wasn't long before everything began to go wrong. There were moments of soaring flight, followed by flappy struggles where the bag bumped along the ground like a saggy party balloon. Managing only to stay a few metres ahead of Jack, the bird finally flapped and sputtered into the cover of a nearby wood, landing behind a big bush.

Jack followed it into the woods, sweating and panting, but by the time he reached the bush the robber pigeon had disappeared. Instead, in the spot where it *should* have been, was a little girl, polishing off his cakes.

'What?' He span around in confusion, looking for the one-legged pigeon. 'Where? Who are you? Give me back my cakes!' He went to snatch them but she, her mouth crammed full of lemon buns, clutched the bag ever tighter.

Jack stared at her, his eyes widening. 'Hang on a minute . . . it's **you**. You're real! You were looking through my bedroom window last night!'

'Wasn't,' she mumbled, gulping down the remaining bits of cake.

'Yes, *yes* you were!' insisted Jack. 'How dare you? You can't just go around scaring people in their beds and stealing their cakes! Who do you think you are?' He stared at her peculiar dungarees and even more peculiar hat, his brain still desperately trying to catch up with his eyes. Who, indeed, *was* she? She looked about his age, but entirely different to anyone he'd ever met.

Picklewitch calmly tipped the remaining crumbs out of the bag and into her mouth, dropping most of them down her front. 'You are a very impolite person.'

Jack looked at the poo on his blazer in disgust – and then with dismay at his watch. 'Oh no,' he howled, 'now I'm going to be late, and on my *first day* too!'

He grabbed his rucksack and broke into a run. 'Whoever you are, this is all your fault,' he shouted over his shoulder. 'I don't know what you want but . . . just get lost – OK? Stay away or . . . or I'll call the police – do you hear?'

The girl stood up and watched Jack disappear down the road until he was nothing but a dot. The cakes had been unusually delicious, and as she thought about them a splendid idea crept into her head. Birds swooped down from the trees and picked the stray lemon crumbs from her dungarees as she pondered. By the time the birds had finished – and they did an excellent job – her mind was made up.

And when Picklewitch had made up her mind, there was simply no unmaking it.

3

Wildest Dreams

Jack sat at his school desk, basking in the warm sunlight that beamed through the tall, latticed windows. He sharpened his new pencils and thought how lucky he was to be at such a prestigious school where everyone was an A* student. He fitted right in, like an acorn fits perfectly into its cup.

His new classroom was exactly as he'd dreamed it would be. The corridors smelled of polish and the floors gleamed. Wooden desks stood in neat rows, antique maps hung on the walls and Latin mottos were painted in gold over the doorways. His form teacher, Professor Bright, was brilliantly clever and wore a black gown just like in the films. There was even a classroom cat called Newton. He snoozed on the windowsill, as orange as a marmalade sunset.

Looking around, Jack thought it was more like an old library than a classroom – no chatter here, only silent study. He glanced shyly over at his gifted classmates, heads bent over their books. He hoped they would want to be his friends. He'd noticed that nobody had actually said hello yet, but that was probably because they were very busy.

Craning his neck, Jack could see that Chan the maths genius was working hard on a complicated equation and Phoebe, the violin prodigy, was composing a symphony, her brow crumpled in a concentrated frown. Sitting next to the overcrowded trophy cabinet was Kalel, busy translating an ancient poem into ten different languages. Astrid, the Junior Astrophysicist of the Year, worked on an essay about the birth of stars, her pencil moving at the speed of light. They were the cream of the crop, the cherry on the cake, the bee's knees – and now, at last, Jack was one of them. Finally, he had found a school where he belonged.

Jack turned to gaze out of the window, across the green, level lawns, at the bubbling fountain and the neatly clipped topiary hedges. There wasn't a weed in sight. Never had he been anywhere so perfectly ordered. In the distance he noticed the school gates, tall and elaborately wrought. Caught by a sudden gust of wind, they swung open, allowing a tumble of leaves to gambol down the driveway like copper kittens.

Jack drifted off into a glorious daydream. He wondered what Chan's house was like. Would he invite him over to tea? He'd never been invited to tea. Would he need to bring his own calculator? Or maybe Phoebe would invite him to a recital? He'd never been to one of those either. Would Kalel teach him a new language? Portuguese would be very useful ...

Jack was so lost in thought that he barely noticed his teacher opening the door and ushering a small person into the room. Abruptly Newton sprang to his paws, fur on end, bristling and hissing.

'Children,' announced Professor Bright to the class. 'Such a surprise! It would seem that we have not one new student starting today, but two!' The little girl standing beside him rocked back and forth on her boot-heels, glaring at Newton through a cracked pair of binoculars.

'No,' Jack whispered, catapulted out of his daydream. 'No-no-no. Nope. Not her – anyone but HER.'

'Yes, class, this is . . .' Professor Bright looked confused for a moment. 'I'm so sorry, I'm afraid I've forgotten your name. What is it?'

The girl reached beneath her pointy hat and,

after a bit of rummaging, pulled out a large leaf. 'My business card,' she announced. Professor Bright took the leaf. It was inscribed with a single word in black mud. Some of the letters were big and some were small, but there was no doubting what it said:

'How odd,' he frowned. 'What exactly is a *picklewitch?*'

The little girl slowly lowered her binoculars, revealing a pair of wicked green eyes. 'Well, *I* is a Picklewitch of course. I would have thought that was obvious. How rude. What a frazzlin' fopdoodle! It won't do, no it won't.' She glared hard at him and said in a firm tone: '*BAMBOOZLE.*'

At this a fat bee flew out of Professor Bright's right ear and did a loop-the-loop. It buzzed away up the corridor, apparently taking the professor's wits with it because he promptly flung his arms in the air and did a little dance. His sharp, eagle eyes became as round and moony as a lovesick owl's. 'Of course! How silly of me. You're the girl with the ... um ... gift!' He scratched his head in confusion. 'Although precisely what it is seems to have slipped my mind too for now. Anyway, welcome, *dearest* Picklewitch! *Welcome* to St Immaculate's School for the Gifted!'

Jack went hot and cold all over. He wanted to shout *'but she's NOT gifted, she's just a MAD BUN THIEF!'* but panic had caused his tongue to go all floppy.

'Now, who would you like to sit next to?' sighed Professor Bright happily, his eyes still wobbling and rolling about. 'Chan? Astrid . . .?'

But Picklewitch didn't need anyone to tell her what to do. She grabbed a desk and dragged it across the classroom, its metal feet screeching over the tiles. Jack tried to make himself invisible, sinking down into his seat as she got closer and closer, until she was *right next to him*.

Picklewitch pulled up a chair and plonked herself down on it, dumping a grubby rucksack on the floor. Jack wrinkled his nose: she smelled strange and earthy, of frosty leaves and mushrooms. 'Phew! Hello again, remember me?' she said in a loud voice, her eyes bright with naughtiness. 'I bet you thought you wouldn't see me again **but here I am! SURPRISE!**'

Jack's mouth flapped like a trout but no sound came out. 'It's all right,' she said, patting his hand. 'You don't need to thank me. From now on we'll stick together because that's what best friends do. Picklewitch and Jack, Jack and Picklewitch, bubble-gum buddies.' She grinned wide, showing a black gap where a tooth should be. 'We'll be like two peas in a pod!'

Blushing furiously, painfully aware that everyone was staring at them, Jack finally managed to spit seven words out in a low whisper: 'You are still ... *dressed* ... like a ... *witch*.'

Picklewitch smiled at him. 'I thought you were supposed to be clever. I am dressed *as* a witch, not *like* a witch. There's a difference. Anyway,' she said, glancing at his red blazer, 'YOU are dressed like a CLOWN.' With this she pinched his nose and it made a parping noise. Picklewitch found this immensely funny and to Jack's horror the other children lowered their books and began to giggle.

'That's not what I mean and you know it!' said Jack through clenched teeth. 'You don't belong here. We aren't friends – I told you to stop following me! You can't sit here. You'll have to leave. You're ... you're not even wearing the right uniform!'

'MY uniform is perfect.' Picklewitch straightened her pointy hat and removed a small feather from her earhole. 'MY uniform's got special features. For example, I have a most excellent spider pocket.' Her eyes brightened. 'Ooo, do you want to see? He's in here somewhere . . .' She stuck her arm deep into the pocket of her dungarees.

'How lovely to see you settling in so quickly, Picklewitch,' smiled Professor Bright, gazing in surprise at the little green fern unfurling in his inkwell. 'It's always easier if you already have a friend.'

'But . . . but . . .' spluttered Jack in desperation. No one was listening. Everyone seemed too busy admiring his strange new 'friend'.

4

Grub

Lunchtime shone like a beacon of hope on the horizon. Jack saw it as an opportunity to put as much distance between himself and Picklewitch as possible. When the bell rang he leapt up and made a dash for the exit. But Picklewitch, moving with lightning speed, met Jack at the door, flashing a mischievous grin.

'Well done, Jack,' called Professor Bright, watering his fern. 'Excellent idea, looking after Picklewitch in the dinner hall. First days are never easy. It's good to have a chum.'

'But she's NOT my *chum*,' muttered Jack, stomping behind Picklewitch as she skipped towards the dinner hall, hat in hand. 'Does she LOOK like my chum? I don't think so.'

Jack chose a table and threw his lunchbox down with a clatter. His classmates sat at various other empty tables nibbling their sandwiches quietly. Moments later Picklewitch sat down and began to rock back and forth on her chair legs, all the while watching his lunchbox with a greedy eye.

'*I* know!' said Picklewitch brightly, breaking the icy silence. 'We could swap lunchboxes.' She said this as if the thought had just occurred to her and it hadn't been her plan all along. 'Do you . . .' she wheedled, licking her lips, 'mayhaps, by any chance, have any more delicious *cake* in that box?'

Jack gripped his lunchbox and glared.

'Listen – I'm not *ever* sharing anything with you *ever*. Got it?'

'Well I think you *should*,' insisted Picklewitch, fluttering her eyelashes, "coz we is friends and sharing is the sort of thing that friends do.'

'How many times do I have to say it? We *is* not – I mean *are* not – friends so NO it is not something we should do.' Jack stared out of the window and clasped his lunchbox to his chest, defiant and enraged.

Picklewitch sighed and hitched up her dungarees. 'Have it your way.' Without further warning she climbed up on to her chair, threw her head back and launched into a loud and colourful song about badgers' bottoms.

Down at Badgers' Bottom
The wind's far down below,

WHIFFLIN' HUMBUG BUMS AHOY!
They gust and there they blow
Eating up the worms and the roots
and other 'orrible stuff
WHIFFLIN' HUMBUG BUMS AHOY!
a magnificent sort of guff
OH high on the mountains
and far across the sea
WHIFFLIN' HUMBUG BUMS AHOY!
but nowhere will you see
The badgers coz they's hidin'
deep below the ground
WHIFFLIN' HUMBUG BUMS AHOY!
trumpy-trumpy sound
OH! Their gizzards is most nasty
They'd make your eyes fair smart
WHIFFLIN' HUMBUG BUMS AHOY!
a magnificent sort of ...

'GET DOWN,' Jack hissed. The polite chatter and clatter of the dining hall had dropped to a whisper. Everyone was staring. 'All right, all right, you can have my lunch. Just *please* shut up.'

'But of course,' she said, stopping promptly. 'That is most kind. Manners is very important to witches.' She clambered down and seized his lunchbox, squealing with delight: it contained two cheese sandwiches cut into triangles, salt and vinegar crisps and – best of all – three little cupcakes topped with pink icing. She shovelled them down like a starving seagull and let out a big burp, dabbling delicately at the corners of her mouth with a napkin.

'There now, that wasn't too hard was it?' said Picklewitch, gleefully pulling her own unopened lunchbox out of her tatty rucksack. 'Now it's your turn. There's lots of yumscious goodies in there.

The cheeky sparrows packed it 'specially for my first day at school.'

Jack looked down at Picklewitch's lunchbox. It appeared to be made out of bits of old nest. Inside, sat on a bed of moss and sheep's wool, were wiggling worms, grubs and seeds. It was all sprinkled with a flurry of broken eggshells. A spider crawled out from underneath and waved a cheerful leg. Jack's rumbling tummy fell silent.

He noticed everyone was looking at him, waiting for his next move and suddenly realised that this could be his big moment; *goodbye* Little Lord Smartypants, *hello* Daring Adventurer. 'There goes Jack,' they might say, 'he's SO brave! We should definitely invite him to our birthday parties.' Jack looked up at the expectant faces and then down at the lunchbox. It twitched and he felt a shudder rattle through him.

'Eat up! Badgers love this stuff and everyone knows they've got lovely shiny claws. Why not start with a little snack?' Picklewitch wrapped a maggot in a leaf and held it up close to Jack's nose. 'Everso good for you.' Jack thought it looked like the very worst sort of sausage roll. 'Unless of course . . .' she wheedled, 'you is afeared.'

'Afeared? Don't be stupid. I'm not scared,' laughed Jack, looking thoroughly scared.

'Well, what's the hold-up then?'

A tide of children rushed in around the table. 'Ugh, Jack, are you really going to eat that?' asked Victoria in disgust.

'Jack, you're so brave,' said Astrid.

'I bet you were a bit of a legend at your last school, eh Jack?' said Angus Pilkington-Storm, thumping him on the back, making Jack splutter.

There was no going back now; he was in too

deep. Jack squeezed his eyes shut, pinched his nose and popped the grisly snack in his mouth. The crowd gasped as he rolled it around, trying to force it down. Picklewitch watched in fascinated delight as Jack's eyes bulged and popped. It wiggled aimlessly around his mouth until he could stand no more and spat it out. The maggot shot across the table like a bullet and landed in a glass of water, to rapturous applause.

Jack wiped his tongue on his blazer amid the screams of disgust and delight. 'Yuk yuk yuk! That was revolting!'

'I know,' called Picklewitch over her shoulder, as she swanned out of the dinner hall. 'I wouldn't dream of touching the stuff.'

5

Fly Away Home

On the way back to the classroom Picklewitch declared herself 'worn-out with study' and swerved into the girls' toilets to play with the 'magic waterfalls and paper streamers'.

Back at his desk Jack found that, for the first time in his life, he couldn't focus on his lessons. Picklewitch's presence was as disturbing as a dirty cobweb in a freshly painted corner. This was not how the first day of his brilliant new life was supposed to go.

He tried very hard to concentrate on his work

but was distracted by a flash of green winding around the edge of the shelves, tendrils slipping between the textbooks. Where had *that* come from? It wasn't there this morning, he was sure of it. He traced the ivy back down the wall, along the floor and up through a draughty crack in the skirting-board. Jack snipped at it crossly with a pair of scissors. 'This Picklewitch person,' he muttered to himself as he yanked it up and threw it in the bin. 'Who is she anyway? Why is she here? Why won't she leave me alone?' He noticed a spiky bramble poking through the window catch and furiously snipped at that too. 'Most importantly: how am I going to get rid of her?' He couldn't face a rerun of the lunchtime shenanigans so Jack spent the rest of the afternoon planning a brilliant and fool-proof escape.

At the jangle of the home-time bell, Jack sprang

up from his seat and sprinted out of the classroom, no time for polite goodbyes. He raced through the emergency exit, leapt over the playground wall and ran down the street. He'd mapped it all out, dodging down a network of alleys and creeping through people's gardens, climbing over fences, all the while checking over his shoulder.

Finally Jack's front gate was in sight. *Mum will know what to do*, he thought, getting his breath back. *She's very sensible, just like me. She'll come to the school and talk to Professor Bright and explain that I don't need the sort of friend who tells lies and steals and is downright weird. Good old mum – she's always on my side. I just need to remain calm and focused. It's all going to be OK.*

Jack peered around a hedge to check the coast was clear. Birds sang, trees rustled in the breeze and there was no sign of the pointy-hatted peril anywhere. He'd given her the slip like a pro. Jack congratulated himself on his undercover skills and considered for a moment the possibility of becoming a famous spy or a government secret agent. Then he decided to count to three and make a dash for it.

'One . . .' he crouched, ready to sprint. 'Two . . .' he looked quickly, side to side.

'Three!' A familiar voice whispered into his ear. 'Psst, who are we hiding from?'

'AAARRGGHH!' Jack leaped into the air, turning to see Picklewitch crouching beside him. 'NO! *Why* are you doing this to me?' Jack shouted. 'What's wrong with you? Leave me alone!'

Picklewitch stood up and sighed. A sparrow settled on her shoulder. 'Jack, I'm afraid that would be most difficultatious.'

'What?' Jack panted, wild-eyed.

'Difficultatious. It means tricky.' Picklewitch casually flicked the sparrow off her shoulder. 'It's a word I invented. I am very good with words.'

Jack controlled the urge to knock her hat off. 'Arggh!' he wailed. 'Why are you even *at* my school? It's a school for the brilliant and gifted. You don't even have a gift!'

'I do.'

'What?'

'I'm magic.'

'Magic isn't real.'

'It is.'

'It isn't. What **do** you *want?*'

Picklewitch paused. '*I wants* ...' she said, looking a bit awkward, 'a friend.'

Jack leapt up and raced across the road. 'Well I don't need a friend,' he said. 'Not like *you,* anyway. Just go home.'

Picklewitch stamped her boot crossly and followed him to the other side. 'But I *am* home.'

Jack felt as if wasps were fighting in his brain. 'No, you are NOT home. Look at this . . .' he shouted, jabbing his finger at the words forged into the iron gates. 'That says Rookery Heights. It is MY home, and it's been in MY family for generations so it can't be your home, can it?'

Jack's mother chose this moment to appear.

'Hey, what's all the shouting about?' She looked at Picklewitch and smiled brightly. 'Jack, have you made a friend already? Oh, that's great! Didn't I tell you everything would be all right?'

Picklewitch sniffed at Jack's mum and straight away her face lit up like a fruit machine. 'Is this the one that makes your cakes?'

'Yes, but . . .'

'Goody. Listen 'ere Ladymum ...' Obediently Jack's mum crouched down and Picklewitch whispered something into her right ear. As she did, out of the other ear flew a silver moth. In an instant his mother's eyes took on a glazed expression and a smile curled at the corners of her mouth. 'I've ... I've made you a fresh batch of raspberry slices,' she murmured, the moth now sitting on the tip of her nose. A delicious smell wafted from the kitchen. 'Would you like

to come in for tea?'

Jack barked 'NO SHE WOULDN'T!' but Picklewitch was too quick for him and moved towards the front steps at speed.

'OI! What did you just say to my mum?' he shouted, running to keep up.

'Nothing for you to worry about,' she said, marching briskly through the front door.

Jack looked down at the trail of muddy footprints and gave a hollow laugh. *Now she's done it*, he thought. His mum only had one strict rule and that was 'no shoes in the house'. Picklewitch would be told off now for sure and it would all be over before it had begun. 'Mum, look what she's done,' said Jack, pointing at the carpet in triumph. 'The hallway's full of mud! Mum, look! Leaves are even falling out of her trouser legs!'

Jack turned around to see his mum picking stray daisies from the driveway and artfully arranging them in her hair. 'Mud?' she said dreamily, her eyes misting over. 'Leaves? Really? I hadn't noticed.' She looked up at the leaden skies as if in a trance. 'What beautiful weather we're having. Can't stop and chat, I must fetch those cakes.' She gave a joyful pirouette and trotted into the kitchen, Jack following in dumbfounded silence.

Picklewitch was already at the table, stripy legs dangling, a tea towel tucked into the front of her dungarees, impatient for cake. Jack's mum picked up a plate of freshly baked raspberry slices and placed them in front of Picklewitch. 'Tuck in,' she said, 'there's plenty more where they came from.' She looked on admiringly, asking questions like 'Are those beetles or hairslides? Such an interesting perfume – what is it?' and 'What's your name again?'

Picklewitch didn't reply because she was too busy stuffing her face, bag and every available pocket full of cakes. Jack answered instead. 'It's PICKLEWITCH,' he growled, 'and she needs to <u>GO AWAY</u>.' His mum nodded and smiled calmly. Jack stood on his tiptoes, right in front of her. 'MUM! Did you hear me? I SAID she has to LEAVE!' He thumped his fist on the table, causing the cups to rattle in their saucers. But his mum didn't even flinch, her face remaining a picture of serenity. It was like Professor Bright all over again. What was wrong with the adults around here?

After tea (and strictly against her son's wishes) Jack's mum gave Picklewitch a guided tour of the house. 'This is the hallway,' she said, 'and this is the sitting room. The house is very old and once belonged to my great aunt, but she died and left it to us in her will. Jack has a room up in the attic that looks over the garden.' She squealed in delight as a thought occurred to her. 'I know! Perhaps you could come for a sleep-over. Do you live far away?'

Picklewitch stopped bouncing up and down on the sofa. 'Not far,' she said, clambering down. 'Quite close in fact. But I'm afraid Boxie houses is most dreadful. I wouldn't get a wink of sleep here because there's no inside wind and it's full of fandangling trumpery.' She yawned and stretched. 'It's getting dark. Bedward to the greenwood. Thanks for the snacks, Ladymum.'

Picklewitch tipped the remaining cakes into her hat, opened the back door and strode out into the darkness.

'What an unusual girl,' smiled Jack's mother, as she scrubbed the muddy footprints out of the carpet. 'Do be sure to ask her over again. She's welcome anytime. I'm just so pleased you've finally found a proper friend.'

6

Worser than Maggot Jam

It had been a very strange and difficult day. Jack lay on bed, his arms crossed over his best NASA pyjamas, brooding miserably on the situation. The move to Rookery Heights had not gone as well as he had hoped. A scholarship, a big house – oh yes, on the surface it had looked like a delicious red apple, but lurking inside was a *maggot* called Picklewitch. It was so unfair; she was ruining everything. He'd worked hard to get into St Immaculate's and he had a reputation for excellence to maintain.

Of course he wanted to make friends during his time there, but not *this* sort of friend. How was he going to make proper friends with her in the way, clinging to him like a stinky old mushroom? Jack needed a friend who was clever and smart, someone serious and ambitious who didn't keep breaking the rules. He especially needed a friend who wasn't raving mad. What he definitely didn't need was Picklewitch.

Jack tried to think sensibly about the situation, once again reminding himself that all problems, if approached logically and methodically, could be resolved. He needed to write a list. He turned his bedside lamp on and wrote down the facts in his journal:

Situation: Stalked by a strange girl in fancy dress.

> Problem: She wants to ruin my life.
>
> Analysis: Why? Reasons unknown. Probable
>   madness.
>
> Complication: Everyone else thinks she's
>   great.

Jack had been bitterly disappointed by the way his mother had welcomed Picklewitch with open arms. She was a doctor, so she was supposed to be clever but instead she'd gone all dreamy and mushy, like she'd got custard for brains. Luckily by bedtime she had been back to her normal self, although mystified by the boot prints on the sofa. And he had expected more from someone as qualified as Professor Bright too, who'd got more degrees than a thermometer. No one except Jack – and Newton the class cat – seemed to be able to see the truth.

The other children thought she was great, even

though she was scruffy and rude and said weird things. He puzzled over this, trying to figure out why. He supposed she *was* quite wild and he knew people liked that sort of thing and *yes* the lunchbox dare and his moment of popularity had been more thrilling than Jack was prepared to admit. But no, the facts were plain and simple: Picklewitch was a problem. A fibber and a fraud and a troublemaker, she was going to get in the way of him finding a proper friend. She had to *go*.

He thought and he thought and gradually a plan emerged. Just like him it was both logical and smart. In fact, it was genius. Jack reached for his journal, tore out a fresh page and began to write a letter, sweeter than cherry pie.

Dear Victoria,

I am writing to say how much I admire you.

I think you are the prettiest and cleverest girl in the whole school. I wish we could be best friends. I would tell you myself only I'm much too shy.

I really love eating cakes and you are a baking champion so I think we would make the perfect partnership. Also, for some reason, I think I am magic so I could make all your cakes rise every time.

We could be bubble-gum buddies. Of course I will be sad not to be Jack's friend any more but really we are better suited to each other. I need a friend that I can really look up to and spend all my time with and he is not the person for me, but you are. You definitely are. Can we sit next to each other? Oh-please-oh-please?

Yours hopefully,

Picklewitch

* * *

The next morning Picklewitch arrived late, completely missing Professor Bright's lecture on 'treating public toilets with respect'. She screeched into class full of complicated explanations about bossy robins and angry magpies. But she needn't have bothered – Professor Bright just smiled dopily at her. Jack rolled his eyes in disgust.

Picklewitch was about to take her seat next to Jack when a voice rang out, bright as a bell: '_Picklewitch_! Oh _Picklewitch_!' A girl on the other side of the classroom waved at her, smiling prettily and holding out a freshly baked cake in her hand.

'Why don't you come and sit over here with me?' said Victoria. 'I've made you a cake!'

Jack held his breath. Victoria Steele, world-class baker and the bossiest girl in the class, had found the secret letter he'd planted in her desk before school.

Picklewitch had never noticed Victoria before. Her eyebrows wriggled as she gave the matter some thought. Then she saw the cake and licked her lips.

'Picklewitch,' coaxed Victoria again, speaking in a strange baby voice, patting the seat next to her 'Over here . . .'

Picklewitch sidled sideways up to Victoria. 'Your cake smells . . . unusual,' she said, her nose twitching.

Victoria handed her the blueberry muffin and flashed a sugary smile that didn't reach her eyes.

'Well, they are very special. These are only for my best friends,' she cooed, 'so there's no need to be shy.' She lowered her voice and pulled Picklewitch so close that she pushed her hat brim back. 'Don't worry about the new boy,' she hissed, her eyes shining greedily. 'Just tell me more about the magic.' Picklewitch shrugged and began to tuck into the muffin.

As Jack watched, he felt the weight of responsibility lift from his shoulders as he realised it was all going to be all right after all. Finally he was free and everyone was happy. All it had taken to get rid of Picklewitch was to establish what she wanted – cake and a friend to provide it – and then give it to her. Job done, simple as sunshine, problem solved. Thanks to his big brain, logic had won the day. As a future scientist he would, of course, record the experiment in his journal for posterity. He might even draw a graph.

But mid-muffin Picklewitch stopped chewing, opened her mouth and spat it out. 'No, no this cake is all wrong. Ugh.' Picklewitch wiped her tongue on her hat brim. 'YUCK and ICK. Worser than maggot jam.'

'How dare you?' gasped Victoria, stamping her little bowed shoe. 'Those muffins won Best Bake of the Year! I'm a very gifted baker! You must like them. *Everyone* says my cakes are the *best* cakes!'

'Really?' Picklewitch raised her eyebrows. 'That *is* a surprise, because Jack's cakes are much friendlier. Witches is most particular about flavours, you see. Unfortunately your blueberries taste bossy and . . .' she rolled her tongue around her mouth . . . 'and your sponge is mean. Thank you and good day.' And with that, Picklewitch scraped her chair back and returned to the seat next to Jack.

Jack banged his head on his desk in despair.

'Come-come, now-now Jack,' said Picklewitch soothingly, wiping her sticky hands on his blazer. 'Don't feel too bad for her – not everyone can have a witch for a best friend.'

7

Stickybeak

Picklewitch was like a wasp or a verruca – she just wouldn't go away. But luckily Jack was no pushover either. He'd read enough about the lives of famous historical figures to know that you didn't get ahead by giving up when things got tricky. Lots of people overcame personal problems and went on to greatness: Elizabeth the First was bald, Beethoven had asthma and Napoleon was scared of cats. Jack's problem was Picklewitch.

'Listen, Newton,' he whispered to the class

cat. 'We both know she isn't gifted – she's a rotten cheat and fibber. I just have to prove it.' Lost in thought, Jack plucked bits of moss off the bookshelf and straightened the crooked antique maps. 'I need to expose her as a fraud and unworthy of a place at the school. *Then* someone will have to listen and she'll be booted out of St Immaculate's forever.'

'Careful what you wish for, that's the last lesson of the day,' said Professor Bright, writing TUTANKHAMUN on the board. 'Treasures? Wealth? Fame? The people who excavated the tomb of Tutankhamun came to believe it was cursed. Please sit down and we'll begin our Egyptian project.'

Excited at the prospect, Jack zoomed over to his chair, pencil poised, ready to learn. Picklewitch's ears had pricked up briefly at the word 'cursed', but it wasn't long before she developed a serious case of The Fidgets. She wriggled and sighed and tutted. She flicked a selection of mixed nuts at the ceiling. Then she pulled a dandelion clock out of her pocket and blew fluff all over Jack's books. When she got fed up with this she moved on to pulling funny faces and telling jokes.

'Psst, Jack. Jack. JACK! What type of tree fits in your hand?' Jack looked straight ahead at the board in stony silence.

'Psst. Jack. Psst. Do you give up? A PALM tree! Geddit?' Jack didn't flinch.

Picklewitch cracked her knuckles and wriggled her eyebrows. 'Jack, Jack, what do you call a witch at the beach? A SAND-wich. Ha-ha!'

Jack counted calmly to ten and picked the dandelion seeds out of his hair. He mouthed two words (SHUT UP) and turned back to the board. Picklewitch sulked for a whole seven seconds before bouncing back with the determination of a kangaroo.

'Jack, excuse me. Jack. Jack. I've got a proper serious question about Tooting-carmoons. It's really very, very important.'

Jack sighed. 'Go on then.'

'What's yellow and smells of bananas? Do you give up? It's monkey sick. MONKEY SICK! A-HA-HA-HA! MONKEY SICK!'

'Jack!' His teacher suddenly appeared, looming over the desk, his eyes like laser beams. 'Are you listening? What did I just say?'

'Oh ... er ... I don't know. Picklewitch was just ...' Jack burbled, full of panic.

'Precisely. You don't know because you weren't paying attention, were you? There's no place for time-wasting *or* disloyalty at St Immaculate's, do you understand?' And with a swish of his black gown Professor Bright returned to the front of the class, like an irritable bat.

'Yes sir, sorry sir,' said Jack, hurling a thunderous look at Picklewitch.

'See what you've gone and done now?' Jack hissed, furiously rearranging his pencils. 'You're such an idiot. I'm sick of you and your ... your *stupidity*. You're messy and a liar and a cheat and a thief and ... and I wish you'd just get lost!'

Picklewitch knitted her eyebrows together and stuck out her bottom lip. 'Well. *That's* not very nice. Moody fopdoodle. Mister Know-It-All. I'm only trying to have some fun. Be a snollygaster an' a weasel an' an all round moaning stampcrab then. I'll take my brilliant sense of humour back where I'm appreciated. You ungrateful ... bloomin' ... *Boxie*.' She grabbed her bag in a mighty huff, opened the window and climbed out.

Jack felt a sharp twist of guilt; he knew it was wrong to be mean. On the other hand he knew that Picklewitch had skin thicker than rhino hide. She'd be back by teatime, when she would no doubt have forgotten all about everything he'd said and be as annoying as ever.

He looked at the clean, blank page in front of him and felt a huge sense of relief wash over his mind. *Finally I can get down to some proper studying. First things first though*, he thought, *I need a nice, neatly underlined title . . .*

One eye on the board, Jack reached down into his rucksack for his new ruler. He expected to feel the familiar rows of neatly filed items but instead his hand plunged into sticky, spiky darkness.

'Urgh! Yuck!' Disgusted, he yanked his hand back out and wiped it on his trousers. He looked down at the bag in confusion – this rucksack was patched and dirty and not at all like his smart one. Suddenly the horrible truth dawned – in her rush to leave, Picklewitch had taken his bag by accident. Full of panic, Jack jumped up and leant out of the window. 'But my lovely things!' he wailed.

'SIT DOWN, JACK.'

'But . . . Picklewitch . . .' Jack protested.

'NOW!' Professor Bright's eyes bulged and his lips quivered in an alarming manner. Jack plonked back down in his seat, teeth clenched at the injustice of it all. It was so unfair; even when she wasn't there she was *still* getting him in trouble. Jack's insides boiled with rage.

He glared down at her tatty bag and a sneaky

thought popped up like a toadstool: *What exactly does she keep in it that's so special to her anyway? She carries it everywhere.* She seemed to know a lot about him, but Jack realised he knew hardly anything about her. Normally he wasn't the sort to pry in another person's private things but today was not a normal day. He looked around – no one was watching – so he dipped a cautious hand back inside and carefully pulled out an exercise book. He laid it on his lap under the desk and inspected it.

It was nothing at all like his own school exercise books, which were plain and smart. The grubby cover was peppered with fruit stickers, snail trails and sooty fingermarks. 'A Gift from the Seaside' was stamped on the back. On the front was one single word, written in Picklewitch's familiar inky scrawl:

GRIM

Grim by name and grim by nature, thought Jack with a snort. He slipped the schoolbook back into the bag and waited eagerly for the bell to signal the end of class. He needed to examine the evidence in secret and he knew the perfect place to do it.

8

Grim

At the back of St Immaculate's was an overgrown cemetery. It was a peaceful, sunny place full birdsong and mossy headstones. Most importantly of all, it would be deserted. As the other children fled out of the classroom and off towards home, Jack hung back in the playground. He waited until the coast was completely clear and then climbed over the wall.

Jack sat in the long grass and took out Picklewitch's exercise book for closer inspection.

The pages were stuck together and prising them apart took some effort but he tugged and tugged until they finally unpeeled.

As Jack scanned page after page of chaotic scribbles and brown stains he felt the tension in his shoulders release. Finally, here was the evidence he had been looking for. *What a load of old rubbish this is,* he thought eagerly. *There's no schoolwork here at all, not even basic maths or spellings. Just wait until Professor Bright sees this, then he'll understand my point of view. After all, it's called St Immaculate's School for the Gifted, not St Immaculate's School for Weirdos. She'll have to move to a different school. He can't argue with hard evidence.*

But, as he continued to turn the pages, one by one, Jack found himself strangely drawn in. There were instructions on how to mend a bee's wing, a collection of leaves with Latin names and a calendar of moon cycles. There was a list entitled 'DANEJERUS PLANTS' and quite a lot of poetry, including one called:

BURD
Slug slime lickings
Harf a thurd
Wish me so
A robber burd

Jack gave the book a cautious sniff. The pages smelled curious and bittersweet, of herbs and smoke, of honey and vinegar. A clipping of a recipe fell out on to the floor. 'What's this?' He bent down and picked it up.

BAMBOOZLE SOUP

Ingredients:

4 fox hairs

9 nettle stings

2 drops of dragon's blood

(strawberry jam if no dragon)

Method:

Stir together well by glim-light and drink from a teapot.

Chant:

Hoodwink the Boxies

Bees and moths and flies

Picklewitch is bestest

BAMBOOZLE ears and eyes.

Difficulty level:

Middling

(Note: will only work if done on Tuesdays and Thursdays)

It sounded like horrible soup; there weren't even any onions or carrots. What was glim-light? Was it a sort of gas hob?

Jack read the recipe again. That word: 'bamboozle'. It wouldn't leave him alone. It niggled and wiggled in his thoughts. *'Look at me'* the word seemed to say; *'here I am'*, as if it was trying to tell him something.

Then Jack remembered: this was the word Picklewitch had said to Professor Bright on her first day. Hadn't she whispered something into his mum's ear too, right before she'd started behaving in that strange way. *Bees and moths and flies?* He pictured the silver moth on the end of his mother's nose. Jack shut the book and looked again at the title.

One of the reasons that Jack was so clever was that he had a remarkable memory and once he learnt something he simply filed it away neatly until it was needed again. 'Grim,' he repeated to himself, the files in his mind shuffling. 'Grim ... I know this word too.' He paced up and down the files in his memory until he found it. 'Aha – got it! The holiday in Cornwall!'

Jack could see the memory in his head, as bright and clear as a star. It had been a sunny day with ice creams and children fishing with nets in the rock pools, but inside the witchcraft museum it had been dark and cold; a tangle of strange corridors and odd objects. It was pretty creepy and he'd been glad to leave. On the way out there had been a big cabinet stacked with old journals. A spooky carved sign hung on the door: *A Collection of Grimoires: Witches' Books of Spells and Secrets.* There were other signs that said variously PRIVATE and *DANGER* and *DO NOT TOUCH.*

Suddenly the pieces of the puzzle locked into place with a terrifying and resounding *click*. Jack dropped the book like a burning coal. 'That isn't a schoolbook and that's not *soup*,' he gasped. 'That's a *spell* – a real SPELL!' It all added up: the bird that stole his cakes, her night-time appearance at the attic window, the outfit, the bizarre behaviour of his mum and Professor Bright, her weird old-fashioned words, the disgusting lunchbox, the terrible attitude and the pointy hat. She even had a missing tooth.

'But that would mean ...' Jack gulped. She couldn't have been a *real* witch all along, could she? *NO. No, no, no. Magic's not real; it's only make-believe*, he thought. *I mean, believing in magic is not logical is it? Real witches are supposed to be old and warty and fly on broomsticks and she's just a little girl so it* can't *be true.*

But it *was* and in his heart he knew it.

Jack forgot all about school as he picked the Grim back up and flicked urgently through it: past recycling lists, carefully compiled fruit stickers, a directory of dewdrops and different breeds of wind beast, a complicated zodiac, then past chapter headings for Air, Earth, Water, Fire and Spirit. They weren't poems or recipes; of course, they were *spells*, hundreds of them! Spells for 'tree balding', spells for lightning, spells for something called 'Kat-Hik-Hups', spells for shrinking and growing, spells for scattering and spells for gathering. Some were written in big letters, some in tiny barely legible type, some swooped in loops around the page and others squatted in corners, as solid and square as a chair. Jack recalled the leaves tumbling through the gates on that first morning, the creeping invasion of ivy and brambles, as if Nature had followed her to school like an obedient pet. He turned to the last page. On it was a stick drawing of a witch perched high in a large tree. She was waving at the attic window of a house.

A cold wind suddenly picked up and the birds fell silent. Jack felt a shiver run down his spine as anxious thoughts began to fall over each other: What was it he had he called her? An idiot? A liar? A cheat? A thief? *Why-oh-why* had he done that? His stomach was gripped into a knot of fear. Jack tried to focus on the pages of the book but now the words seeped in and out of the paper like water and he began to feel sick.

A blast of low autumn sunlight burst out from behind the clouds, carving sharply between the headstones. Jack blinked and squinted, dazzled by the bright glare. He rubbed his eyes and, when he looked again, a sharp, triangular shadow stood over him. It grew and grew, spreading out like a black inky stain until it filled his vision to the edges, plunging the day into night. He felt the ground throb beneath him as the whirring of wings got closer and closer. His nostrils filled with a thick, smoky stench of bonfires and black, wet earth. Jack tried to say something, to explain, to plead, but no sound would come out. He dropped the book, hid behind his arms and waited for the worst ...

It took Jack a while before he was brave enough to peek out, but when he did so he was amazed to discover that everything was back to normal. The birds twittered cheerfully and the gentle sun shone down on the daisies. He looked around for the book but it was gone and Jack didn't wait to find out where. He scrambled to his feet, jumped the wall and *ran*.

* * *

All the way home, his legs pounding like pistons, Jack was in a daze. What had just happened? Was it real? Had that been her? She had felt so different. Beads of sweat broke out on his forehead as he remembered the witchcraft museum signs again. He should <u>not</u> have looked in her book of spells. He ran past the school, past the playground, his brain racing. He'd read enough fairytales to know that crossing a witch was a bad idea. 'What if she decides to put a curse on me?' he fretted. 'She's got loads of spells in there. What if she turns me into a toad? Or a weed?'

Finally running out of breath, Jack slowed to a walk as he got nearer to home and his thoughts began to settle down.

Perhaps I'm getting this all out of proportion, he thought. *Maybe it's not as bad as all that. She might be a twenty-first-century witch but she's still just a little girl. Maybe I could tell her I was joking and perhaps she'll see the funny side. She's always saying what a great sense of humour she has. Or I could just be nice from now on and she'll forgive me for spying on her. I could explain it's all been a misunderstanding. Or I could pretend that I believed her all along and everything will be all right.* 'Yes,' Jack said to himself, as he walked up the gravel drive of Rookery Heights and opened the front door, 'that's a good plan. I'll explain everything later.'

But Picklewitch didn't come back later. Or the next day, or the next. Picklewitch disappeared as mysteriously as she had arrived.

9

One for Sorrow

The days went by and St Immaculate's returned to its old self. In the classroom the ivy died back and the fern in Professor Bright's inkwell turned brown and wilted. Mysterious draughts and leaves disappeared from the corridors and the snails stopped eating the books. Silent study returned to the school once more.

Without Picklewitch in it, Jack's life ran like clockwork again. His blazer stayed clean and his mum bought him a brand new bag. Now that the chair next to him was empty he could concentrate in lessons and his work was always finished to perfection. At no time was he turned into a toad or a weed and he didn't have to share his lunchbox with anyone. He won the class weekly award for Punctuality and Presentation and Professor Bright put gold stars next to his name in the register. Even Rookery Heights was starting to feel more like home. Jack had got exactly what he had wished for, but he felt oddly flat.

He found himself searching for Picklewitch in the playground and in the toilets at breaktimes. He looked for evidence that she had been nearby – leaves, muddy footprints, floods, rambling plants, possible explosions – but there were none. Occasionally one of the other children would come over and want to know where his funny friend had gone but all Jack could do was shrug. Where *had* she gone? And why hadn't she come back? It felt unfair because he was going to explain but she hadn't even given him the chance.

A week passed and Jack sat alone on the playground wall. 'She was a pain,' he reasoned, unwrapping his single portion of cake, 'but now I know she's supposed to be like that, maybe she's not really *so* bad. I mean witches are known for their bad behaviour and some of her jokes were quite good I suppose.' The fact was she was fun and everyone knew it. The school was a friendlier place with Picklewitch in it. He thought about how she could make the whole class laugh, just with a look. It really was a gift.

Jack was brilliant at lots of things, but making friends didn't seem to be one of them. It wasn't easy, like calculus or quantum equations, it was tricky and he'd never been sure how to go about it.

This had always made him sad, because his mum said his heart was in the right place.

But for some inexplicable reason Picklewitch, who could have picked anyone in the whole school as a best friend, including bossy Victoria, had chosen *him*.

As the days went by, Jack became increasingly distracted in class, wondering where she had gone. Sometimes he whispered her name out loud, just in case she was hiding nearby and might spring out at him as a surprise. He secretly watered the skirting-board and kept the classroom window ajar. On his journeys to and from school, Jack found himself walking slower than usual, taking notes, keeping a half-eye out for one-legged pigeons or stray cake wrappers. He slept with the attic curtains wide open, just in case she wanted a midnight chat. He even wrote jokes in the mist on the window in case they made her laugh, but she never came to read them.

Jack thought about his beloved collection of ammonites, in rows on his bedroom shelf, next to his Lego and his model planes. *Meeting Picklewitch was a bit like stumbling across an impossible fossil and throwing it away,* he thought sadly. How could he have been so stupid? He could kick himself. 'Sometimes, Jack,' he said to himself as he turned off the bedroom light and looked out at the moon, 'you're not half as clever as you think.'

Then, just when he was beginning to wonder if he might have imagined the whole thing, Picklewitch came back.

10

Witchfinder

On the afternoon that Picklewitch swept back into his life, Jack was busy making a mental list of all the capital cities of the world in alphabetical order. Walking home alone, he opened the creaky gate and crunched down the driveway. He was chanting 'Vienna, Washington, Zagreb' when something caught his eye. Stuffed into a rosebush, he spotted his long-lost school bag! But now it had a word written on the front in mud:

Jack span around, expecting to see a cross little face topped with a bird's nest of hair. 'Picklewitch? PICKLEWITCH!' There was no reply, other than the sound of rooks cawing at each other from trees. On the driveway, hopping from foot to foot and eyeballing him in an accusing manner was a magpie. Jack remembered the magpie superstition 'one for sorrow'. He fumbled with the front door latch, dashed up the stairs and shut the bedroom door firmly behind him.

Sat on his bed, Jack didn't know what to do next. The word 'traitor' was not encouraging. *But surely*, he reasoned, *if she were going to turn me into something, she'd have done it by now?* He took out his journal and listed his options:

1)	Tell a grown-up that I have crossed a witch.

He looked at the words for a moment and sighed. *That sounds bonkers*, he thought. *Also, I'll have to explain why and then they'll go looking for her and I'll get into trouble for spying on someone's private things.* He scribbled it out.

2)	Run away and hide at the North Pole.

Jack considered the idea and concluded that he didn't fancy being a polar bear's dinner, so he crossed that out too.

3)	Find her and say sorry.

Jack had looked almost everywhere: the park, the playground, the school, the shopping centre, the library, the swimming pool, even the cemetery. There was only one possible place left. Jack stood up, crossed over to the window and looked down into the gloom of the garden below.

The walled garden at Rookery Heights still gave Jack the collywobbles and, so far, he had managed to avoid it. He stood very still for a moment and eyed the door. It was now or never. 'Just do it, Jack,' he said out loud to himself, summoning all his courage. He wrapped himself in a thick coat, marched down the stairs, grabbed a cake from the kitchen and picked up a precautionary cricket bat from the hall cupboard.

Jack kicked hard at the rickety garden door and

squeezed through the narrow gap. As he did so a piercing wind raised the alarm, shrieking through the trees like a guard's whistle.

'Picklewitch!' Jack called, his voice higher than normal. 'Where are you?' He smashed and hacked his way through the brambles and nettles in the semi-darkness with the cricket bat, trying not to think of vampires and monsters. Leaves crunched under foot and twigs cracked and snapped, as loud as breaking bones. He stepped in something squishy and winced.

'Picklewitch,' he squeaked, brushing cobwebs from his face. 'I know you're there. I've come to say sorry!' He wound his way through the undergrowth as it closed in on him, dark and savage. Thoughts began to bubble over: *What if I can't find my way out? What if a branch falls on my head? Who said that? What if something bites me? Where is she? What am I doing out here?* Panic gripped his thudding heart: 'PICKLEWITCH! PICKLEWITCH!'

An owl shrieked and Jack shrieked back, whipping his cricket bat around. In the scramble he slipped and fell flat on his back – SPLAT – into a muddy puddle.

Gasping for breath and terrified, he looked up to find himself beneath the canopy of a large walnut tree, bright stars appearing between its branches, moths fluttering in the light cast from the moon. As his eyes focused he could see boot soles, attached to a pair of stripy legs, dangling down from a branch.

'Picklewitch!' he cried in relief. 'THERE you are! What are you doing up a tree?'

'Silly question,' she said, sulkily. 'I live 'ere, don't I? Who wouldn't want to live in the most

beautifulest and magnificent tree in the world? Should've stayed in it too. A more cleverer question would be what is you doing down there, lying in the dirt like a great fat sneaky worm?'

Jack scrambled to his feet. He noticed that Picklewitch was rubbing her tummy and scowling. Birds were roosting on her shoulders and pecking at her hat, much to her annoyance. 'Gerroff! Always pecking and picking. I'm not a fudge-frazzlin' birdfeeder. Leave me alone.' She flapped her arms to scare them away, but three more blackbirds landed on her hat. Jack had never heard birds giggle before.

She was clearly not in the best of moods so Jack thought it was best to come straight to the point. 'I want to say how sorry I am, Picklewitch,' repeated Jack, in his most polite voice, which he usually reserved for librarians and policemen.

'Sorry? SORRY, is it now? YOU took your time.' Picklewitch took a deep breath. Jack knew she was about to say something bad in the same way you know that a thundercloud is going to burst and everyone is going to get wet. He wished he'd brought an umbrella as well as the cricket bat.

'YOU is a traitorous Boxie fudgenut, that's what. YOU has not been a good friend to Picklewitch. You has been unkind.' She wiped the corner of her eye with her sleeve, pretending she'd got something in it. 'Friend Rule Number One: friends don't spy on friends – that's lower than a snake's tummy button. Rule number two: friends believe friends when they say they is a witch.'

'Sorry.'

'THREE: You don't not NEVER EVER touch a witch's special things. NOT NEVER.

Even the squirrels know that and they're as thick as porridge.' She was standing up now, her hair bright and wild against the moon. 'You think you're clever but you're not. You're a grubbler and a ... and a gobberlotcher.'

'Sorry,' repeated Jack.

'My Grim,' she thundered, waving about her book, 'thinks I should turn you into a cat with wonky eyes and a sausage for a tail. Or mayhaps you'd prefer the voice of a crow? Caw-caw! Eh? That'll learn you and then you won't be so keen to go poking your dozypox fudgefrazzlin' Boxie beak where it don't belong.'

Jack felt anxious. This was not going as well as he had hoped.

'But,' she said, her mood suddenly brightening, 'I shan't. Luckily for you witches only bear a grudges 97 per cent of the time. Grudges is bad manners and manners is very important to a Picklewitch.' She folded her hands in her lap, as prim as a governess.

Phew, thought Jack. It was time to eat humble-pie before the wind changed again. 'I am really very, *very* sorry, Picklewitch. I shouldn't have looked in your bag; it was very rude. I'm really not a traitorous fudgenut, honestly, and I want to be a better friend. Please don't do anything bad to me. I'm really sorry I hurt your feelings.' Jack looked awkward. 'Could we start again, now we understand each other better? I've ... I've missed you.'

'*For example*,' breezed Picklewitch, as if she hadn't heard him, 'it would be bad manners to visit a friend's beautiful home and not bring a delicious something.' She folded her arms and wiggled her eyebrows. But Jack was ready for her.

He reached into his pocket, pulled out a chocolate cupcake and held it up in the air.

A magpie swooped out of the tree, snatched the cake out of Jack's hand and delivered it into Picklewitch's waiting palm.

'But maybe you shouldn't eat it if you have a tummy ache . . .'

Picklewitch crammed it all in her mouth and spluttered, 'Don't worry, all better now.'

'So,' Jack called up into the branches, 'will you be coming to school tomorrow?' Darkness was falling fast and Jack was keen to go back to the safety of the house.

'Mayhaps, if you're going to go *on and on* about it,' she said. 'They're probably missing me I s'pose. Birds are driving me potty anyway. I could do with a bit of peace.'

'See you tomorrow by the front gate then?

8.30 sharp?' Jack called up. 'A fresh start? Even-stevens? Fair and square?' he added hopefully. 'Oh, and please don't bamboozle my mum again because that's not on. And maybe tomorrow you could leave the pointed hat at home?'

But Picklewitch didn't answer because she was already fast asleep and snoring, chocolate icing on her nose and a bat swinging from her boot-heel.

11

Science and Spanglechuff

Jack was so excited at the prospect of:

a) having a best friend

b) having a real witch for a best friend

c) not waking up cackling like a crow

that he hardly slept a wink thinking about all the brilliant adventures that two especially gifted children could have together. The sky was the limit. The next morning he got up bright and early to wait by the front gate.

8.30 came and went but still there was no sign of Picklewitch. Jack checked his watch: if they left now they would only just make it in time. '*Come on*, Picklewitch,' he whispered impatiently as another minute passed. *Maybe witches are always late*, he thought, tapping his foot. *Maybe I should go to her tree?* He could give it a bit of a shake and she might fall out like a walnut. Two more minutes passed. He decided that he would have to explain that rules were there for a reason. He could teach her all sorts of things; Jack was full of good advice. He looked at his watch again. Where was she?

Jack waited as long as he could – until the very last possible second – but Picklewitch didn't come. Jack sprinted all the way to the school gates. As he burst into the classroom, his hair sticking up and his tie askew, the first person he saw was Picklewitch. She was sitting studiously at their desk, her nose in an upside-down book.

'Ah, Jack,' frowned Professor Bright, watering the fern that had mysteriously recovered overnight. 'At St Immaculate's

I'm afraid we take a very dim view of lateness.'
He took two of Jack's stars out of the
register and put them next to Picklewitch's
name. 'Perhaps you should look to your friend for
a good example.'

Jack sat next to Picklewitch in a huff. 'Why
didn't you wait for me?'

'Ah,' she said sweetly, licking her palm and
smoothing down her hair. 'I forgot to say: witches
don't wait.' He paused for her to say sorry, but she
didn't. Jack looked down at her desk and noticed
that her pencil case looked exactly like *his* missing
pencil case. In fact, ALL the things on her desk –
calculator, pens, rubber, colouring pencils, ruler
and compass – were all his. Jack was deciding
whether he should say something about this, when
Picklewitch said, 'Cheer up, because it's science
this morning and I am excellent at science.'

'Are you? Are you really?' Pleasantly surprised, Jack perked up immediately. He had a real passion for physics, chemistry and biology, not to mention geology, archaeology and astronomy. He had lots of science textbooks at home and hoped one day to become a famous scientist and discover something really important. He even had a t-shirt that said 'Science Matters' on the front. Maybe this was something they would have in common. Maybe they could be a witch and boy super-science duo.

'Oh yes,' said Picklewitch, flicking a paper ball at Newton's twitching tail. 'Witches is absolutely whizz-cracking at science. Just you wait and see.'

* * *

Professor Bunsen was a world-renowned Lepidoptorist and the author of the bestselling textbook *The Butterfly Mind*. He took science lessons at St Immaculate's. He was very serious and there was a school rumour that he had never smiled, not even once. Jack worshipped him like a god.

'Today, children, we will begin with a discussion on weather systems. Who can tell me about them?' A sea of hands shot up in response and Jack was no exception. He thrust his hand in the air. Where should he start? With the rainforest? Or with the Arctic? Should he talk about the moon's magnetic field or simply start with hurricanes?

Professor Bunsen frowned and pointed at Picklewitch. 'You – new girl.'

Picklewitch coughed a word that sounded very like 'Bamboozle' and Jack shot her a sharp look.

'That question is too easy.' She sighed, crossing

her boots on the desk. 'The weather is the job of Barnacle Whisper: the bear what does live on the moon.'

The class roared with laughter. But Jack knew it wasn't a joke. Picklewitch *meant* it and he felt his insides shrivel with embarrassment.

'Very amusing, Miss . . . er . . .' Professor Bunsen looked at the register. 'Miss Witch. Does anyone else have an intelligent answer?'

Picklewitch got to her feet and pointed a filthy finger at the teacher. 'Now you listen to me, Barnacle does all the storms, and the droughts and he's especially good at fog. He's won prizes for his mists.' She began a full coughing fit: 'BAMBOOZLE-BAMBOOZLE-BAMBOOZLE!'

Professor Bunsen tutted and turned to ask one of the Wilson twins instead.

At this moment, Picklewitch spotted the antique display cabinets mounted on the wall.

'Well that explains it,' she said, pointing at the butterfly collections. 'Such wicked fandanglery right under our very noses. That's why bamboozle's not working,' she muttered. 'This one's a dark wizard all right.'

'He's not a wizard,' hissed Jack. 'He's a scientist, which is actually much better. Don't worry, those butterflies have been in those cabinets for centuries.' Dr Bunsen disappeared into the science equipment cupboard to gather trays of beakers, clattering and rattling. 'Look,' said Jack, changing the subject, 'we're going to do an experiment!'

Picklewitch thought for a moment. 'Do you mean a spell? Can he do magic?'

'In a way,' said Jack in an excited whisper.

'He can do things like make erupting volcanoes with bicarbonate of soda and vinegar.'

Picklewitch arched an eyebrow. 'Can he turn that desk into a giraffe?'

'Well, no of course not. Scientists can't do that sort of thing. Shhh.'

'So they *can't* do magic?'

'Well ... er ...'

'Watch this ...'

'NO PICKLEWITCH NO!'

But it was too late. She whipped a feather out of her pocket and sneezed over it: '*SPANGLECHUFF!*'

An icy wind whistled through the classroom, caught the science cupboard door and slammed it shut, turning the lock. 'Who did that?' Professor Bunsen shouted from inside the cupboard, rattling the handle. 'Open this door at once!'

Up on the wall the keys of the display cabinets fell to the floor with a clatter and the doors swung open on their hinges. To everyone's confusion they now stood empty. 'Where have the butterflies gone?' demanded Jack. He narrowed his eyes and glared at Picklewitch: 'Put. Them. Back.'

'Back?' asked Picklewitch, her smile as innocent as a sunbeam. 'I'm sure I do not know to what you are referring.'

Suddenly there was a lot of screaming as butterflies began to erupt from the children's uniforms. Hundreds of butterflies – Monarchs, Peacocks, Brimstones and Painted Ladies – poured out of pockets and sleeves, fluttering through the air like rainbow confetti. There was a mad dash for the door, causing a crush as everyone tried to escape the flappy mayhem.

'What have you done?' shouted Jack over the chaos. Picklewitch stood serene, adorned in butterflies. She shrugged, sending them off into the air. 'I'm not exactly sure how it happened. Sometimes things just *occur* when I'm cross. I need to write this one down because this really is an excellent and unexpected result . . .'

'Excellent? EXCELLENT?' Jack's mouth hung open. He looked at the empty cabinets. The science cupboard door rattled and shook with increasing force and he could hear Professor Bunsen's bellows. 'What am I supposed to do about him?'

'Dark wizards get what they deserve. Anyway, it's cooking next and I'm *really* looking forwards to that. See you there, Friend!' She gave an enthusiastic wave and disappeared through the classroom door, leaving Jack to make feeble explanations through the science cupboard keyhole.

It took Jack most of break time to calm Professor Bunsen down and persuade the caretaker to call a locksmith. When he finally made it into the playground there were only a couple of minutes left. Straight away he spotted a large crowd in the corner, the sort that gathered only when something big was happening. His stomach lurched as he spotted Picklewitch in the centre, the star of the show.

'You *see*,' she explained, smiling at the attentive crowd, 'there's three types of magic: Middling, Massive and Megatronic. ALL of my magic is

Megatronic, *naturally*.' She gave a little bow, with a flourish for dramatic effect.

'But how did do you do it?' marvelled a girl with curly hair, pushing her way to the front. 'How did all the butterflies get from the cabinets into our pockets? It was amazing!'

'It was better than amazing,' laughed Chan. 'It was miraculous! It's not been the same without you here, Picklewitch. You make everything more fun! Can you do some magic for us now?'

'Oh go on,' said another child wistfully. 'It must be brilliant to have magic as a gift. All I can do is speak seven languages fluently and play the flugelhorn.'

'Oh well,' cooed Picklewitch, tickled by the attention. 'If you insist. It's mostly down to practise, you see.' She gleefully rubbed her hands together as her eyes settled on some worms in a playground puddle. 'Now, how about I turn those worms into pythons?'

Jack marched into the middle of the crowd and grabbed Picklewitch by the elbow. 'Ha-ha, she's just joking! We're not in the Dark Ages, are we? Of *course* she can't do real magic, that would be ridiculous! These performances are perfectly explainable – this is the twenty-first century, after all!' he said over his shoulder, as he dragged her away. 'It's all sleight of hand. She's just a gifted magician; you know, like the Great Umbonzo or something. That's what the costume's for ...' he pointed at her hat. 'Very theatrical, you see. It's important to look right – it's all part of the act. You're more of an illusionist, aren't you Picklewitch?'

Picklewitch fought him off, her arms waving like a windmill. 'No I am not! Theatrical? How very dare you! I AM A POWERFUL, MOST EXCELLENT WITCH! I've got a certificate! Gerroff you ... you *STINKFUNGUS!*'

The crowd gradually dispersed but Victoria lingered behind, casting vinegarish glances at Picklewitch and noting things down in a little book. 'What you looking at, Bossy Baker?' shouted Picklewitch, pointing her crooked finger. 'You'd better watch it, Missy, or there'll be a-bamboozling before bedtime!'

Jack dragged Picklewitch with some difficulty over to the corner of the netball court for a private chat.

'Listen, Picklewitch. This has got to stop. YOU know you can do magic and *I* know you can do magic but you've got to stop bamboozling people. You definitely can't go telling everyone you can do real magic.'

'And why would that be, Mister Cleverclogs?' Picklewitch folded her arms, her eyes narrowing into green slits. 'Mayhaps you're just jealous.' She stuck out her bottom lip in a sulk. 'Everyone else has a talent: thingy with his fancy words and wotsit with his flugelhorn. Why can't they know I'm magic?'

This was a good question and one that Jack had sat up half the night worrying about. The fact was that people didn't like witches. He knew from history books that for centuries they'd got the blame for everything from crop failure to the milk going off. Soldiers burnt down their houses and even ducked them in ponds to see if they would drown. Angry villagers would chase them with pitchforks – they were called witch-hunts for a reason. But how could he tell Picklewitch that? She'd only get into a froth about it.

He was also smart enough to know that if grown-ups got to hear that there was a real witch in the school, there would be endless trouble. They'd have to make it official with forms and inspectors, they'd interfere with what-ifs and whys and have lots of serious questions about health and safety. Even if she *hadn't* been magic they wouldn't let a little girl live alone in a garden with just the birds to take care of her. They would probably take her away from her tree. What if they even experimented on her? She had only left the safety of the garden because she wanted to be his friend. A friend wouldn't let that happen to another friend.

He thought about Victoria's note-taking and suddenly remembered the letter he'd put in her desk, the one that was supposedly from Picklewitch, confessing she really *was* magic.

Jack felt a stab of shame. No one else must ever know. It *had* to remain a secret because then he could keep her safe. Friendship was so much more complicated than he'd ever imagined, especially when that friend happened to be a witch.

Jack took a deep breath and said the kindest, cleverest thing he could think of: 'You're right, Picklewitch, I AM jealous. I've never had a special friend like you. Can't it be our secret? Wouldn't that be fun? Please don't tell anybody else about the spells and stuff. It could be a special secret between friends: *best* friends. Jack and Picklewitch, Picklewitch and Jack: bubble-gum buddies? What do you say?' He gave her a big smile.

As if by magic all of the fury went out of Picklewitch, like air rushing out of a blow-up mattress. She glowed with pleasure and peered coyly at him through her grubby binoculars. His plan worked like a charm.

12

Hotbox Hiccup

Picklewitch sat in the cookery lesson, her tummy full of warm, friendly feelings. She was on her very best behaviour; putting her apron on neatly, sitting sensibly at the desk, hands folded in her lap and chatting away. She'd even taken her pointed hat off and put a chef's one on instead, just like everyone else. 'I'm not going to use any magic, Jack, I promise,' she said, ignoring the row of birds staring at her from the window ledge. 'I'm just going to cook like a normal human person ...' She pointed over at the saucepans on top of the oven. 'In the happy hotbox. Can we use those pannikins too? Picklewitch loves pannikins.'

Jack managed a smile. Picklewitch was very funny when she was behaving herself. She made up words, like 'flatterator' for iron or 'numberfumbler' for a calculator. He had tried correcting her but she pretended she couldn't hear him. Picklewitch was going to take a lot of work, but Jack loved a project. He would teach her how to behave, maybe recording all of their experiences in a notebook entitled 'How to Fix a Witch'. Maybe he would become a famous writer one day.

Madame Flambé, the Cookery Mistress, stood at the front of the class and wrote on the board. She was a firm Frenchwoman with a small head and long body. Whenever Jack looked at her he was reminded of a rolling pin.

'Today, *mes enfants*, we will be baking Firework Fancies. So-called because they have a secret ingredient – spicy, fiery ginger!' said Madame Flambé. 'They are very warming, with enough spice to blow off your hat – pouff!' Madame Flambé wagged her finger at the class and continued. 'These *magnifique petit* cakes were created by one of our own; a former head-boy of St Immaculate's who now works as the Head Chef at The Ritz, so I will be expecting spectacular results.'

Jack quickly partnered up with Picklewitch. 'I'll be in charge of the ingredients,' he said, 'because it's very important to weigh them out precisely and to follow instructions properly. You can be the mixer.'

Picklewitch seized on the task with great enthusiasm, clouds of flour rising into the air until, by the end, she was white-haired and red in the face from the effort. When it was all mixed together, Picklewitch dipped her finger into the mixture and tasted it. Her nose wrinkled. 'This is wrong.'

Jack laughed at her confused expression. 'They're not ready yet, silly – the mixture has to be cooked, *then* they'll taste delicious. It's the magic of baking. You'll see.'

Feeling relaxed and looking forwards to the results of their hard work, Jack went to fetch the baking tray. It was fun teaching Picklewitch about things, especially as she had so much to learn. Baking was like science and if all the preparation and measurements were right, then the results were guaranteed – a good lesson for Picklewitch to learn!

When he came back, he found Picklewitch leaning over the bowl and muttering something into the mixture.

Jack was immediately suspicious. 'What are you doing?'

'Nothing,' trilled Picklewitch in surprise. 'Nothing-nothing! Can we put them in the happy hotbox now? I'm starving . . .'

It took precisely ten minutes for their oven to explode. It began with a few sparks, then a whizz, a fizz and a crack. Finally there was an enormous boom and smoke filled the air. The whole class was evacuated, coughing and spluttering into the playground. Victoria looked furious. Her hair had been blown out of its neat plaits and now stuck out, a sooty starburst around her head.

Jack listened in shock as Picklewitch patiently explained her actions to him: 'If a cake has the name "firework" in it then it's *supposed* to explode, isn't it? Otherwise what's the point? Ginger won't

do it. Ginger's just a tingle on the tongue. All I did was add a big dollop of the proper stuff to make them go with a bang. She said she wanted to see spectacular results so that's what she got. You'd think she'd be more pleased.'

Madame Flambé, shouting over the sounds of fire-bells and sirens, dragged Jack off to his first ever detention. Here he was made to write 'Gunpowder is not an ingredient' in Latin (*Pulvis ignis pars non est*) four hundred times while Picklewitch stood outside the window making faces at him, starlings picking burnt bits of cake out of her hair.

On the way home, smouldering school in the distance, Jack and Picklewitch visited the local library. Picklewitch was delighted by the natural history section and stripped the shelves bare looking for tree pictures.

While she was occupied, Jack slipped down a different aisle to search for instructional books on friendship. Books normally had the answer he was looking for and not having had much experience in this area, he wondered if he was doing something wrong. He was trying very hard (for example he hadn't said anything when he noticed that she had hacked all the school topiary chess pieces into pointed hats) but was friendship really supposed to be this difficult? Finally he found one called *Best Friends Are Great*. Jack frowned doubtfully; so far he would describe being friends with Picklewitch as more 'risky' than 'great'. There were chapters on listening and sharing but nowhere did it mention witch-wrangling. He sighed, putting it back on the shelf before anyone noticed. He was just going to have to try harder.

The next day Professor Bright announced he had an exciting new project for them. 'After yesterday's troubles, the head has decided that it would be a good idea to get you out in the fresh air. I wholeheartedly agree, having lately having been *seized* with a sudden passion for Nature.' He plucked a buttercup from his inkwell and tucked it thoughtfully behind his ear. He pointed up at the walls, where black-and-white class photographs hung. 'Many of these very pupils went on to became pioneers in their field, some of them exploring Antarctica or even sailing down the Amazon in a canoe. We must never forget that St Immaculate's is a school founded on the quest for knowledge and there is more to life than sitting inside studying in the dark!' The class let out a loud cheer and Jack spied Picklewitch looking suspiciously pleased with herself.

'An independent, curious spirit,' continued Professor Bright, 'is the key to adventure! We want you to begin your own adventures by rolling up your sleeves, getting out of the classroom and becoming Nature explorers yourselves.' He began handing out clipboards. 'Your challenge is to choose a nearby location and perform an in-depth study of its flora and fauna. You will work in pairs and have one week to complete the project. This special prize will be awarded for the best report.' He held up a wooden box full of bamboo tubes: 'A bug hotel!' There was a general gasp of excitement and the scramble for partners began.

Picklewitch's eyes sparkled. She reached into her spider pocket and brought out a massive creepy-crawly. 'Did you hear that?' she cooed at the spider 'A hotel – that's proper posh.' She turned to Jack and looked at him matter-of-factly.

'*I* want that and I'm going to get it and *you're* going to help me because that's what friends do.'

Jack gazed wistfully over at a girl sitting in the corner of the room. Tamsin was a prize-winning environmentalist and would have made the perfect partner. She was always pond-dipping and talking about compost. Tamsin was very particular about technical data, which Jack approved of, but Victoria was already sidling up to her and trying to tempt her with a pastry. He looked back at Picklewitch and bit his lip. 'All right then,' he said, thinking about the advice in the *Best Friends Are Great* book, 'but what location shall we choose?'

Picklewitch stood up, popped the spider back in her pocket and laughed. 'Well that's obvious – the most beautifulest garden in the whole wide world, of course. Follow me!'

13

Two for Joy

Jack had to admit that the garden looked slightly less terrifying in the bright morning sunshine.

Picklewitch clambered through the wild and rambling undergrowth, pushing aside the hawthorn and honeysuckle and bindweed. Jack stayed one step behind, notebook and pencil at the ready.

'I can't wait,' enthused Picklewitch, her hair peppered with thorns. 'It's going to be the best project ever. Now, let's start with listing the most important things: **the trees**. First and best: the mighty walnut!' With a hop, skip and a joyful leap she bounded up into its branches. 'Now, Jack, are you listening?' She held up her hand, five fingers splayed out like a starfish. 'Five top facts about my tree:

1) Its Latin name is *Juglans regia*.
2) Its walnut husks make beautiful brown ink. It is the best spell ink and is extremely magical.
3) It is 157 years old and the oldest tree in the garden.
4) Walnuts are very good for the brain, which is why I am so wise.
5) Walnuts are the best tree of all the trees and my tree is the best of the lot. This fact – fact five – is the most important fact of the five facts. Write that down.'

Jack watched her, his pencil poised. The dark colours of her outfit were camouflaged against the bark and moss. She looked perfectly at home, as wild as a bird.

'Do you live up there all the time, Picklewitch? Don't you get wet when it rains?'

She lifted her binoculars to her eyes. 'Rain's good for you.'

'But what about in the winter. Don't you get cold?'

'Cold's good for you too. Are you going to ask me something about my tree?'

'All right. How long have you lived in the tree?'

'Let me see . . .' she answered breezily, waving a stick. 'Longer than a vole's nose, shorter than an elephant's tusk.' Then, without warning, she dropped out of the branches and trotted off into a bramble patch. Jack called after her.

'Picklewitch ... ow ... spiky ... aarrgh ... but *why* do you live in my garden? Ouch.'

'I live in MY garden,' Picklewitch's voice came out of the middle of the thicket, 'because it's the best place of all. I'd have thought that was as plain as the nose on your face. Now, come and see my treasures.'

Picklewitch dragged a bench out of a bush. 'This was once sat on by a *real* duchess. It's a bit wobbly now, because she had a very big bottom, but isn't it the most special bench you have ever seen?' Jack cast a doubtful eye over the rotten slats and the rust.

'And that,' Picklewitch continued, gleefully pointing at the skeleton of a glasshouse, 'is where the juicy pineapples and peaches grow.' Jack inspected it for signs of fruit, but it was just full of nettles and brambles.

Searching around the back of the glasshouse Jack stumbled across a pair of life-sized stone peacocks. They were lying on their side, their wings chipped, their beaks broken.

'I like these,' he said, picking off bits of moss. 'Shame they're so worn out. I bet they looked impressive when they were new.'

'New?' Picklewitch cocked her head on one side, as if she was unfamiliar with the word. Then she closed her eyes and began to hum:

Wind and weather
Friend and foe
Stone and feather
Alive-alive-O

The stone peacocks began to rock from side to side until they righted themselves. Then their colour began to change, from a dull granite grey to brilliant, shimmering blues and greens. Jack stared open-mouthed as their kaleidoscopic tails fanned out, a hundred bold eyes staring back at him. Like garden royalty, the peacocks slowly strutted away, their sequinned plumage dazzling in the sunlight.

Jack gasped in amazement. 'How did you do that?'

Picklewitch shrugged as if the answer was obvious. 'It's just Old Magic. That's nothing, watch this.' She stuck two fingers in her mouth and let out an ear-splitting whistle. A kestrel plummeted down from the sky and alighted on the ground in front of them.

Picklewitch gave a smart little bow and said, 'Good morning, Kenneth.' Then she raised herself up on tiptoe and began to spin, faster

and faster. A corkscrew blur, she got smaller and smaller, teenier and tinier, until she was no bigger than a field mouse. She hopped on to the kestrel's back and grabbed tiny fistfuls of feathers. 'To the treetops please!' she squeaked. With a squeeze of her stripy knees they soared up, up, up into the sky, leaving Jack waving on the ground, far below. Before Jack could say 'safety regulations' she was back again, full-sized and clutching a single, perfect pinecone for their project.

'That was INCREDIBLE,' laughed Jack, unable to believe his eyes. 'That was the best thing I have ever seen in my life!'

Picklewitch dusted herself off and handed Jack the pinecone for safekeeping. 'Yes, well, it's risky. Sometimes Kenneth's a bit too fond of small creatures, if you know what I mean. Anyway, come and see the sundial . . .'

That morning Jack and Picklewitch were busier than the busiest of bees, zooming around the garden, collecting information in the sunshine. They measured rainfall in a rusty tin bucket and found four different kinds of water beetle inside. They counted the spots on ladybirds' wings, categorised moths and butterflies and rubbed soothing dock leaves on their nettle stings. Seeds were carefully recorded, leaves were collected and woodlice were logged. Picklewitch and Jack worked together, different but the same, two sides of a coin, rolling along. They were the king and queen of the garden and they could do whatever they wanted. They jumped and climbed and splashed and laughed and hid.

* * *

At lunchtime they both climbed up into the walnut tree. Jack opened his lunchbox and took out a fat paper bag of cakes to share. They sat down together on a branch, as friendly as a pair of doves, swapping secrets.

'Squirrels have ticklish knees,' whispered Picklewitch.

'Sometimes my arms get worn out from polishing all my school medals,' confessed Jack.

'Daffodils make me sneeze,' said Picklewitch.

'I love liquorice laces,' said Jack.

'I once made a cat woof for a week,' said Picklewitch.

'This is brilliant, isn't it?' Jack said, his face full of smiles. It sounded as if he was talking about the project but really he meant something else: having a best friend really *was* great. It was much better than playing alone; having a friend was happiness squared. 'I love it here!' he shouted, raising his arms to the sky. 'This is the best tree ever!'

'Told you,' said Picklewitch, appearing next to him on the branch. She tossed a grubby fistful of walnuts into her mouth and crunched them whole.

* * *

Time flew and by the end of the week Jack had gathered a huge file of information. 'The Rookery Garden Project' was indexed and alphabetised, with graphs, pie charts and detailed descriptions of the flora and fauna. Jack had used a whole pack of highlighter pens and his ruler and protractor had never been busier.

Picklewitch hadn't been interested in the actual writing part but Jack was more than happy to handle that; in fact, he decided it was for the best. Handing the finished project in, Jack secretly hoped it would be turned into a reference book. On top of this, Jack felt that he and Picklewitch had really turned a corner in their friendship.

They were a perfect partnership; her with her magic and him with his eye for detail and order.

On Monday morning Professor Bright stood by his desk, his hand resting on the top of a teetering pile of nature projects beside him, ready to announce the winners. Jack glanced over at Tamsin and Victoria, who looked confident. He transferred his gaze to Picklewitch, who was tickling her own nose with a feather and Jack couldn't help but smile. He looked around the class to see everyone else smiling too, ties slightly askew, the room alive with laughter. Somehow, by just being there she'd managed to make the school a brighter place. *It's hard to believe I used to find her so annoying,* he thought. *It feels as if we've been friends forever.*

Sparkling with anticipation, Jack's eyes swept up and down the tower of projects. He'd put it in a red folder so it should have been quite easy to spot.

'That's strange – I can't see it,' he whispered to Picklewitch, craning his neck. 'Can you?'

'Oh it's there,' she said breezily, 'but it's not in that silly red folder any more.'

Jack's heart stopped and his good mood instantly evaporated. 'What do you mean?'

'It wasn't right, so I changed it.'

Jack turned and stared hard at her. He knew that it was important in moments of crisis to stay calm. 'But I spent hours working on it. What do you mean, you *changed it?*'

'Well, *you see,*' she patiently explained, 'in the end it wasn't like the garden at all, was it? It as all very numbery and it felt wrong and the garden thought so too. So last night I made a better one instead.' She sneezed loudly and her feather drifted away.

Before Jack could say anything else, Professor Bright pulled a large sheet of paper out of the pile and held it up for the class to see. In place of the neat list of trees, shrubs and animals that Jack had so carefully compiled, was a raggedy map of the garden at Rookery Heights, drawn in brown ink and covered in stains. In the centre was a drawing of a big tree, full of birds. To emphasise this further it said 'TOO MANY BURDS' next to it. Large areas of the map were clearly marked out as 'Stabby', 'Spiky' and 'Squishy' and one bush in a far corner was simply labelled BEWARE. It listed several plants that Jack had never heard of, which were described as 'gud for aykes and paynes'. There was an arrow pointing behind the potting shed which said STORM BEEST. All of the Latin names had been crossed out and instead plants were named things like 'Cuckoo Bread' and

STORM BEEST
BEWARE
bug hotel NOW
BELOVED of TORTOISE
CUCKOO BREAD
STABBY
TOO MANY BURDS
gud for aykes and paynes
DO NOT SAVIDGE ME KENNETH
SQUISHY
spiky
PRESHUS

'Beloved of Tortoise'. Other features included a recipe for walnut ink, a cluster of spindly insects carrying a banner which said 'bug hotel NOW!' and a whole area labelled PRESHUS', dedicated to recycled milk bottles and stickers. Down at the bottom was a picture of tiny Picklewitch shaking her fist at a fierce-looking kestrel, which simply read 'DO NOT SAVIDGE ME KENNETH'.

Jack struggled to find the words. 'What have you done?' he hissed at Picklewitch 'It's messy and ... and ... stupid and unscientific! He'll hate it!' Jack shook his head miserably. 'This is very, very bad.'

'This,' beamed Professor Bright looking at the map, 'is very, very good. In fact, I would go as far as to say that it has flashes of creative genius.' He held it up for everyone to see. 'Spelling mistakes aside, the creators took our suggestion and produced something original, imaginative and environmentally aware. Professor Bunsen preferred Victoria and Tamsin's project on *The Ecology of the Playground Drain*, but ultimately he was outvoted by myself and Headmistress Silk. This is exactly the sort of thing we expect from such unusually gifted students and is a fine example of Art and Nature working together in perfect harmony. So with no further ado, I'm delighted to tell you that the winners – with their magnificent project – are *Picklewitch and Jack*! Please come to the front to collect your prize.' Everyone clapped and cheered – except for Victoria, who was busy glaring at poor old Tamsin.

Professor Bright handed Picklewitch the prize – the bug hotel, and when he stuck a gold star sticker on to her map she nearly busted her buttons with pride. Everyone clapped and said how marvellous it was and wasn't Jack lucky to have such a funny, clever, creative friend? Jack smiled through his teeth and gripped his chair until his knuckles went white.

14

Mugswoggling Misery

Jack realised he had spoken too soon. It should have been obvious that being best friends with a witch spelled nothing but trouble. He recorded the evidence in his journal:

Tuesday: Rubbish day. Opened my locker and
hundreds of liquorice laces fell out all
over the floor. Note pinned inside door
said:
Gift frum Picklewitch

P.s I did not steel all of the tuk shop
    likkerish 4 U
PP.s This is A LYE!
    Tried to put them back but was too late.
    Professor Bunsen caught me in the act.
    Detention.
Wednesday: Bad day. Picklewitch filled Victoria's
    desk with newts. Everybody laughed (except
    for Victoria who screamed the place down).
    I got in trouble for 'inappropriate use of
    amphibians'.
Thursday: Terrible day. Picklewitch told me she
    was sorry about the newts so had done
    'something to cheer me up'. School Librarian
    furious after she found my name written
    in all the books. Detention for vandalism.
Friday: Disastrous day. Picklewitch climbed on
    to the slippery roof to dance with the

magpies. Whole school watched and cheered her on. Tried to stop her but Professor Bunsen saw me climbing up the drainpipe. Got a detention for Dangerous Behaviour. SO UNFAIR.

Saturday: Hid in my room with the curtains shut while Picklewitch threw walnuts at my window. Maybe next week will be better.

* * *

But as time went by things just seemed to get even worse. Jack noticed that all the teachers were beginning to look at him oddly. When he offered to run an errand they said 'no thank you' or simply laughed in a nervous fashion. He was no longer asked to take the register to the office, or put on monitor duty, and if he made the slightest mistake everyone pointed it out. Where there used to be gold stars against his name now there were just lots of black marks. Somehow he had become one of the 'naughty boys' and it was through no fault of his own.

Picklewitch, however, couldn't have been more popular. She organised a packed-out lunchtime Nature Club with special walnut shell membership badges and told funny stories about the birds that everyone loved. She performed a series of 'unbelievable' magic tricks in assembly that made everyone gasp and clap. Some of the children stopped brushing their hair and started putting bits of lichen and feathers in it so they looked like her. Professor Bunsen gave her the Achiever Cup to take home for the term and new birthday party invitations appeared on her desk daily. Everybody wanted to be friends with the funny little girl in the witch costume. She was having the time of her life and didn't have to bamboozle anyone at all. Meanwhile 'naughty' Jack was about as popular as measles.

One afternoon, as they walked home together, Jack stomped down the pavement, hands thrust deep in his pockets and his head down. Picklewitch skipped alongside, recalling how much Professor Bright had laughed at her hilarious squirrel joke when, for the first time, she noticed that he looked downright miserable.

'What's wrong with you?' she demanded. 'You've got a face like a wet haddock.'

Jack stopped at the gates to Rookery Heights. He turned on his heel and glared at her. 'What's wrong?' He couldn't believe his ears. 'Some friend you are! Do you really not understand? What's *wrong* is that SOMEONE keeps getting *me* into trouble!'

Picklewitch wiggled her eyebrows and frowned.

'Oh no. Oh dear.' She pulled out her Grim, licked a grubby finger and flicked through the pages. The hedgerow, brimful of birds, gossiped and twittered. 'Oh yes. They're saying that this could be the work of an evil mugswoggling wind,' she said looking up. 'Or a hobbledehoy or mayhaps even a hornswangle!'

'Ha-ha. Very funny.' Jack pushed open the gate and trudged into the house, too fed up to argue.

'Cheer up, Jack,' Picklewitch called after him, waving her spell book. 'Friends watch out for each other. You can rely on Picklewitch to sort things out, never fear!'

Jack scowled and slammed the front door behind him. With friends like Picklewitch, who needed enemies?

15

Catnapper

Jack lay awake much of the night tossing and turning, having nightmares about the Picklewitch problem. 'Why on earth did I think it would be a good idea to be friends with a witch?' he fretted as doubts marched around his brain. 'No wonder people used to steer clear of them. I must have been mad.'

By the time the sun peeked over the garden wall the next morning, Jack was decided. He'd had enough; he didn't want to be friends with her any more. He'd tried his best and done everything the books had suggested – being patient, being caring, listening, sharing – but it was just *too hard* being friends with a witch. He was fed up, more unpopular than ever and at this rate he was going to get expelled too.

Jack summoned all his courage. He'd just have to tell her straight out and if she didn't like it – well, tough luck. He got up and went out into the garden to look for her, but when he got to her tree it was empty. Secretly relieved, Jack ran all the way to school alone.

* * *

When he arrived in class the room was buzzing with activity. 'What's going on?' asked Jack, looking around. Everyone had their felt-tips out making posters.

'It's Newton!' said Aamir, his eyes shining with drama. 'He's disappeared – we don't know whether he's been STOLEN or maybe just run away.'

Jack's sharp mind sprang into action as he assessed the evidence. Newton, a very fat cat, was unlikely to have run anywhere. In fact, he had never even left the school playground, having been there since he was a kitten. He must have been stolen. 'Poor Newton!' said Jack. ' This really is *terrible*.' At least it wasn't Jack's fault for once, which made him feel relieved, guilty and hugely cheered, all at the same time.

Victoria slunk over to his desk, as sly-eyed as a fox. 'Where's that witch girl? I'll bet she's at the bottom of this,' she said.

'What do you mean?'

'Well, you know,' she winked, 'witches, broomsticks and . . . well . . . *cats?*'

In spite of everything Jack still felt the need to

stick up for Picklewitch. She might be a pain but he wasn't going to give Victoria the satisfaction of admitting it. 'Don't be stupid, Victoria. I've told you, she only *pretends* to be a witch and she certainly doesn't own a broomstick. If you knew her at all you'd know she doesn't even like cats.'

Victoria flounced off and Jack got straight to work. He drew up a detailed chart, listing all possible options and the probability of Newton being found. Jack formed an official search party and together they stuck up posters on lampposts and on walls, scouring the school for evidence, such as a bit of orange fur or a paw print, possible signs of a scratchy struggle.

But, despite all their hard work, Newton was nowhere to be found. 'Somebody must have seen him,' insisted Jack. 'What a mystery!' Even though he hadn't cracked the case just yet, he felt very pleased with himself for the first time in days because, without Picklewitch muddying the waters, he knew he was doing a good job.

Just before lunch, Headmistress Silk put her head around the classroom door. 'Excuse me, Professor Bright, I'd like to speak with Jack in my office.'

Jack sat bolt upright in his chair. The headteacher of St Immaculate's only wanted to see you in her office if you had been *very* good or *very* bad. His eyes swept anxiously around the room to see if Picklewitch had reappeared, but she hadn't, so he felt instantly reassured.

As Jack trotted down the corridor after the Headmistress he imagined that she must have seen his investigative efforts and wanted to congratulate him. After all, it was so important to be thorough in a difficult case such as this.

He'd given up on being a witch-fixer so maybe he would become a detective when he grew up, maybe even the head of Scotland Yard. He was feeling so much more cheerful than when he had woken up that morning, almost back to his old self. *What a difference a few hours can make,* thought Jack.

The Headmistress opened her office door to reveal a surprise: a growling orange cat sat in the arms of a grumpy police officer.

'Newton!' Jack cried in delight. 'There you are! What brilliant news. Those posters have worked quicker than I thought. Where have you been?' Jack grinned and grinned, right up to the point where he noticed he was the only one wearing a smile.

'Please sit down, Jack,' instructed Headmistress Silk. Jack did as he was told and she handed him a letter. It was written in a familiar scrawl and Jack felt his blood run cold.

I, Jak (bestest friend to Picklewitch)
do solemnly declare that
the Kat called NeWTuN is
the most terribul TRUBBLEMAKER,
FLEABAG, SNITCH and SPY.
I have arrested him an am delivering
him to you
to throw into JAYL for a hundred
years.
Signed Jak Door

Jack blinked in disbelief. 'But ... but ... I didn't write this! You've got to believe me! That's not my writing – that's not even how I spell my name!'

The Headmistress shook her head in dismay.

'I wish I could believe you, Jack, but let's look at your recent behaviour, shall we?' She balanced a pair of reading glasses on the tip of her nose and opened a file. 'Locking Professor Bunsen in the science cupboard, blowing up the cookery room, vandalism, misuse of amphibians, dangerous behaviour, theft ... and now animal abduction. Lying will only make it worse.' She lowered her spectacles. 'This is very disappointing.' Jack crumpled at the use of the D word.

'Young man,' said the police officer, 'I do not have time to be arresting cats. We have human criminals to catch.' His uniform was covered in enough hair to knit an orange poncho.

Jack tried to concentrate but he was distracted by a black pointy hat, bobbing up and down outside the window. Newton caught sight of it too and bolted with a hiss.

'I'm afraid, Jack,' continued Mrs Silk, 'we cannot tolerate this sort of behaviour at St Immaculate's. We are a school that celebrates *excellence*, not bad behaviour. Therefore I can only recommend ... **that you should be expelled.**'

'No!' Jack sprang to his feet, his eyes pricking with panicky tears. This couldn't be happening; it was too much! Leave St Immaculate's School for the Gifted? The bottom would fall out of his world! The idea of being sent back to his old school filled him with dread. 'Please *no*, Headmistress,' he wailed, clutching at his scarlet blazer. 'I ... I can explain!'

But Jack knew he couldn't explain, so he resorted to begging instead. 'Please, I promise nothing like this will ever happen again. I'll do anything – please give me another chance; there's been a terrible misunderstanding. I won't let you down. You have to believe me. *Please.*'

The head frowned at him for a long moment and, eventually, her face relaxed a little. 'You do seem very sorry, I suppose, and I must admit that we had such high hopes for you. Your scholarship scores were among the highest we've ever seen.' She took a leaflet out of her drawer and placed it on the desk in front of him. 'I am going to give you one last chance, one big challenge to prove yourself worthy of your place in the school.'

Jack picked up the leaflet in front of him.

25th Interschool End of Term Quiz Championship – Entries Open

Headmistress Silk escorted him firmly towards the door. 'Put together a winning team.' She pointed at the calendar. 'You have two weeks to prepare and show me that you are the sort of pupil that St Immaculate's can be proud of. Bring the victory cup home where it belongs, Jack. Or else.' The door closed behind him with a firm click.

Jack's heart leapt; *of course* he knew about the quiz! St Immaculate's had entered a team every year ever since it began, twenty-five years ago – it was legendary and the highlight of the school year. He also knew that twenty-four winner trophies stood in the school cabinet. With so many brilliant children in the school it was the greatest honour the school had to offer and the responsibility was huge. Captaining the team was his dream come true. Jack felt as if he'd escaped from the shark's jaws and somehow landed in a sea of fabulous chocolate instead.

He looked up to see Picklewitch peeking

around the corner at the end of the corridor giving him the thumbs-up sign. Jack wanted to strangle and hug her at the same time.

'Shame they brought Newton back, but he's learnt his lesson, just like that dark wizard,' said Picklewitch conversationally as they walked back to class. 'As soon as you said someone was getting you into trouble I knew you was talking about that cat. First day at school, "Picklewitch" I sez to myself, "that orange moggy's a spy and a traitor." Did you know that cats eats birds? Actually EATS 'em with their faces! My word, he's a frazzlin' fudgeknuckle and everyone knows it.' She gave a big wink. 'Couldn't hear what was going on in there but I wanted them to think it was all your idea, so I was clever and left the note. Brains, see?' She tapped her finger on her head 'S'all right, you don't need to thank me. I ain't no fairweather friend, I'll stick by you Jack, come rain or shine.'

Jack looked at her eager, proud face. How could he tell her he didn't want to be her friend? The words stuck in his throat like a fishbone. Friendship was turning out to be a lot trickier than the books had led him to believe. He marvelled at Picklewitch's ability to land in a bed of roses – it was a gift. Sour and sweet, she really *was* a pickle. Nevertheless, the fact was that, thanks to her, he was bound for glory once more. He just needed to keep the news of the quiz a secret for a *little* bit longer.

* * *

Professor Bright was waiting for them at the classroom door, his face a picture of smiles.

'Congratulations,' he said, pumping Jack's hand up and down. 'That's quite a turnaround.' He looked up at the class 'Everyone: Jack's going to be the new Captain of the End of Term Quiz Team!' Everyone stood up and gave Jack a round of applause. 'Good news travels fast,' winked Professor Bright. 'Don't let us down. Picking the right team will be a difficult task.'

Picklewitch's eyes sparkled with excitement and she clapped her grubby hands with glee. 'A team? For a squiz? Well, Jack, why didn't you say? That's really good news because I'm brilliant at squizzes. I knows lots of stuff. I knows how to hypnotise a hedgehog and how many birds can fit in a bin lid. I can even play the recorder with my nose.'

Jack gritted his teeth and smiled politely. He needed a plan and this time it had to be witch-proof.

16

The Kipper's Knickers

The audition queue for the Interschool Quiz was very, very long and Jack had never been more popular. 'Pick me, Jack, pick me!' Every child in the school was a genius of sorts, so Jack was spoilt for choice, but there were only five places and in the end he settled on a dream team of four plus himself. Jack wrote down their names in his book:

Astrid Olsen: Astrophysicist and mathematician from Sweden. Has discovered a planet. Very serious and brilliant.

Angus Pilkinton-Storm: Olympic hopeful and sporting genius. Big, jolly and kind.
Aamir Patel: Greek scholar. Speaks eight languages. Shy, small, brainiac.
Fenella O'Shaunessy: Author. Published five books on Shakespeare by the time she was eight. Clever but sobby.

They were exactly the sort of friends he had hoped to meet on his first day – staggeringly clever, organised, talented and smartly dressed. They were his kind of people. He printed out the list and pinned it up on the school noticeboard. A crowd gathered around and Picklewitch pushed her way to the front and inspected it closely, her nose pressed to the paper.

'This is wrong.' She jabbed a finger at the list.

'Because my name's not on it.'

Jack pulled her to one side and lowered his voice to a whisper. 'I'm sorry Picklewitch, I couldn't include you. You're just too, er, too . . .' Steam began to curl out of Picklewitch's nose. Her eyebrows knotted in a dangerous manner. Jack could see a tantrum building from her boots up.

'Now ... er ... Picklewitch, don't be like that. I can explain. You see, it's because you are ... *too* clever. In fact, you are *so* clever, that if you were on the team we might even get disqualified. Let's not forget you're a true witch. We just can't take the risk. Think of the school.'

Picklewitch huffed and puffed. She sulked and she sighed but in the end had to agree that Jack was right, she *was* too clever. After all, Professor Bright had called her a genius and given her a gold star. Facts were facts.

'I think I'd better sit in on your practices though, just to make sure you're studying the right things, don't you?'

'Oh yes, that would be very useful,' said Jack doubtfully. 'You must come. Definitely.'

At their first practice session the very next day, Picklewitch popped up with the determination of a thistle. Jack took her to one side and handed her a pile of books.

'Wassat?' she asked suspiciously.

'These are for you, Picklewitch.'

'What do they do?'

'Animals appear in them.' He lowered his voice to a whisper. '*They are highly magical.*'

'What sort of highly magical?'

'Numerology: magic numbers.'

She turned the book upside down and flicked through the pages and gave it a shake.

'Pfft. What, no spells? That sounds most unusual.'

'Yes, but this IS most unusual. All you have to do is join up the numbers with this er ... enchanted scribe ... and the magic will appear before your very eyes.' Jack handed her a pencil and gently guided her into another room, closing the door behind her.

Picklewitch loved the pile of dot-to-dot books. Consequently two weeks passed without Jack getting into trouble even once – it was bliss. The quiz team practised and practised in the library until they were pitch perfect. They knew all the capitals of the world, every breed of dog, every river. They could confidently list all of Bach's symphonies and do complicated mathematical equations on the spot. The basics of nanotechnology were in the bag as well as the Latin for gorilla (*Gorilla gorilla*).

They were ready to blaze their way to glory for the twenty-fifth year in a row.

Late in the term, on the evening before the quiz, Fenella brought in a toy owl. 'It's a mascot,' she explained with glee. 'It's to bring us luck. Owls are clever and studious, just like us, you see?' she hugged it close and her eyes welled up. 'I call him Mr Snuggles.'

Picklewitch popped up from behind a bookcase, making Jack jump.

'No,' said Picklewitch, grabbing Mr Snuggles and dumping him into the wastepaper bin. 'No, no, no. OWLS is NOT good luck nor clever neither; ask any bird and they'll tell you. They pretend they know it all but their brain is full of whiffle-waffle. All owls is good at is STARING.' Picklewitch did a funny impression, which made Angus laugh. Fenella's bottom lip wobbled.

'Fiddlededee,' sighed Picklewitch, rolling her eyes. 'I thought you lot were supposed to be clever. Think about it – owls even say "twit". In fact, it's 50 per cent of *everything* they say. What *you* need is a badger. I can get you a real one if you want. He's called Basher Crunch and he's due out of jail any day now.'

'No thank you,' said Jack quickly, rescuing

Mr Snuggles from the bin and handing him back to Fenella. 'That won't be necessary.'

Then Picklewitch had a brainwave: 'I know, why don't *I* be your mascot?' Her eyes shone at the thought.

'Actually,' said Aamir, pushing his glasses back up his nose, 'the word *mascot* originally comes from *masco*. It's Italian for *little witch*.'

'SEE?' said Picklewitch. 'That proves it. Everyone knows witches is lucky. Witches is the kipper's knickers.'

Angus grinned. 'That sounds like a great idea. We could do with a bit of magic! Welcome to the team!' he said and gave Picklewitch a high five that knocked her sideways. Jack felt panic rising in his chest. This wasn't supposed to happen; he hadn't thought about the mascot angle. He needed to think quickly because

Picklewitch could *definitely not* come. When it came to critically important school quizzes she was not the kipper's knickers, whatever they were. She was a spanner in the works, the fly in the ointment, the hair in the soup. Jack thought fast and said the first thing that came into his head. He knew his mum would agree. 'Er ... the thing is Picklewitch, my mum is making a BIG celebration cake tomorrow, just in case we win. In fact, she was saying to me how much she needed your help,' he added, lying through his teeth and feeling traitorous.

'A big cake? Me?' Picklewitch licked her lips.

'Yes. A really, *really* big cake.' Now Jack had started, he might as well carry on. 'It will have cream and jam and icing and silver balls and sprinkles and chocolate.'

'Really?' Picklewitch's eyes span like saucers.

'Yes,' said Jack, sensing he was on to a winner, 'and it will be as high as your head.'

Picklewitch began to drool. 'That is certainly important work. Sorry, team, but I've got other plans now.' She rubbed her tummy and Jack breathed a big sigh of relief. The idea of Picklewitch as their mascot made him feel quite dizzy, and not in a fun way.

The next morning as the minibus pulled away, crammed full of singing St Immaculate's staff and pupils, Jack straightened his tie, checked his seatbelt and relaxed into his seat. Finally – he was going to lead his team to victory, win back his good reputation and Picklewitch, safely at home in the kitchen, couldn't stop him.

But Jack's excitement was tinged with guilt. Picklewitch would probably have enjoyed a day out, he thought, as the countryside zoomed past the window, but he couldn't take the risk of her ruining his chances. He had to do this alone. Looking around at the packed minibus, the teachers squashed into the front singing the school anthem, full of end-of-term jollity, flowers in their lapels, he consoled himself with the fact there weren't any spaces left anyway. Eventually Jack relaxed and smiled to himself. 'There isn't even any inside wind and Picklewitch *certainly* wouldn't like that!'

* * *

But luckily, up on the roof of the minibus there was *plenty* of wind. Holding on to her hat and waving at the passing cars, Picklewitch was having a high old time.

17

Quiz Swizz

On arrival at the stadium, Jack could see the car park was full of minibuses. Schools had travelled from the four corners of the British Isles. There were so many different school crests: dragons, eagles, unicorns and castles. 'Wow!' said Astrid, spotting a rainbow of school flags, 'That's a lot of competition!'

'Everybody wants that shiny cup,' said Jack seriously, 'so remember, team – it's our job to hold on to it.'

Teachers from the different schools greeted

each other and shook hands, their gowns and scarves flapping in the wind like black sails. They were as excited as the children, looking forwards to the holidays, waving their arms and chanting old school songs.

Finally the formalities were over with – name badges were pinned on, ties straightened and hair brushed – and it was time to get down to business. The teams were directed to the big hall where the first knockout round was to be held. The lights were dimmed and everyone took their seats, ready to begin. In a hot flash all the lights went up and the quizmaster ran on stage to a roar of applause.

'Welcome, one and all, to the twenty-fifth Interschool End of Term Quiz Championship Knockout! Stay calm, work together and remember: knowledge is key! May the best team win!' With this a bell rang out and the playoffs began.

For the first time in ages, Jack felt perfectly at ease. His nerves dissolved and the team galloped through the questions to cheers from their school friends. Nothing was too difficult for them. The national animal of China? Easy. The largest desert on Earth? Simple. They were on fire with cleverness, they sizzled with skills. Before long, St Immaculate's had won all three of their heats and swiftly moved up the rankings into the semis.

The competition blazed on as, one by one, schools were knocked out. Before long they were whittled down to just two teams and one of them was St Immaculate's. Jack, Fenella, Angus, Aamir and Astrid hopped up and down in their seats, high fiving and whooping, delighted at their performance. Jack really *had* put together a remarkable team and Mrs Silk was clapping so hard Jack worried her arms might drop off. Her warm smile beamed across the room and finally, Jack began to believe that his worries were behind him.

'Ah, again – the astonishing St Immaculate's!' said the quizmaster, joining them at their table. 'I can't say I'm surprised to see you in the final, but many congratulations on what has been an outstanding performance so far. Please follow me to the finalists' common room where you will be introduced to your final opponents.' He gestured down a corridor.

As the team trotted after him, they all discussed who the other finalists might be.

'I wonder if it will be The Lantern School? Or Phoenix Prep?' Aamir piped up. 'They've got some brilliant minds on their team.'

Astrid twiddled her plaits thoughtfully.

'Possibly St Peter's? They were exceptional on quadratic equations.'

'I bet it's Riverside School,' sighed Fenella in admiration as they plonked down into the comfortable chairs. 'Now there's a team worth beating.'

'Let me see,' said the quizmaster, running his finger down the list on his clipboard. 'You will be facing . . .' he stopped and peered at the list. 'Well! How unexpected *and* in their first year too – the Brutus Academy of Saints & Heroes.' Bewildered, Jack looked at his teammates. B.A.S.H? No – they hadn't heard of them either. 'Ah, here they are now,' said the quizmaster, hearing footsteps in the corridor. 'I'll leave you to get to know each other a little better. Back in a moment.'

As the quizmaster left the room, the team from Brutus entered. Jack held out his hand politely.

'Hello, pleasure to meet you. We're the team from . . .' But before he could say any more the Brutus team captain grabbed Jack by his tie.

'Shut it. I don't care where you're from,' sneered the boy. 'I'm Rupert Pinspike and all I need to know is that you're WIMPS and LOSERS.' He turned to the huge boy at his side 'Tell them what happens to losers, Barry.'

Barry looked confused. He stopped snapping the complimentary pencils for a moment. 'Erm . . . um . . . do they lose?' He tossed a rubber in the air and munched it like a peanut.

Pinspike rolled his eyes in despair and turned his attention back to Jack. 'Now, listen carefully to me, you bunch of wimpy swots.' He pressed his nose against Jack's so hard that their eyeballs were nearly touching. Jack noticed that the Brutus crest on his blazer pocket featured a hammer. 'The only thing you're going to be gifted at today is losing, do you understand? L.O.S.I.N.G. Brutus ALWAYS wins.' The rest of his team began to stamp their feet and beat their chests like gorillas, grunting 'BASH! BASH! BASH!'

Pinspike released his grip on Jack's tie, pushing him back down into a chair and knocking Aamir's glasses off in the process. Another two boys picked up Astrid's bag and threw it around the room until her calculator fell out.

'Please be careful,' complained Astrid. 'That's my fourth-best scientific calculator.' The Brutus boys guffawed, picked it up and chucked it out of the window, narrowly missing a one-legged pigeon perched on the sill.

Jack knew he should say something. Fenella was trembling like a whippet and even big Angus was frozen to the spot. They'd never met anyone who used their fists instead of their brains. It was shocking and for once they were all lost for words.

At that moment the quizmaster popped his head around the doorframe and instantly the team from Brutus were all cheery grins. 'Made friends? Are you all ready to begin?' asked the quizmaster. He spotted Jack's worried expression and chirped. 'Nothing to fear, St Immaculate's. It's only a quiz!'

Pinspike looked back at the quaking gang, 'Yes, of course, *it's only a quiz*.' Barry cracked his knuckles and Fenella let out a small whimper. 'May the best team win,' said Pinspike. He clicked his fingers as the rest of his team lumbered after him down the corridor.

Jack's team stood, shell-shocked. After a long silence Angus turned to Jack and whispered, 'They don't look much like saints and heroes to me. You're the captain. What are we going to do?'

'We'll have to *lose*, of course,' interjected Astrid, anxiously tightening her plaits. 'You saw what they did to my calculator. What do you think they'll do to us if we win? They'll pulverise us. They'll smash us into smithereens. We're thinkers, not fighters.'

'She's right.' Aamir neatly folded his glasses and put them in his blazer pocket. 'I'm sorry, Jack, but they are simply too menacing. These glasses are new and my mother will be super-cross if they get broken.'

Fenella said nothing, just clutched Mr Snuggles and gazed mournfully down at Astrid's smashed calculator in the car park below.

Jack felt a powerful rush of loneliness. Suddenly he missed Picklewitch terribly and wished more than anything that she was there – Picklewitch would have stood by him until the ends of the earth. Small but mighty, she wasn't the sort to give in to bullies; *she* wasn't afraid of anyone. But like a fool he'd sent her away when he needed her most. Thanks to him and his stupid witch-proof plan, she was at home merrily sticking silver balls on to a winners' cake that wasn't even going to be needed. Picklewitch *would* have made a better mascot, certainly better than any twit of an owl.

I'm an idiot, he thought. *No, worse, I'm a rubbish friend and a ... a* fudgenut *and if I don't come up with something fast I'm going to be an expelled fudgenut too.* Then he had an idea: a speech! He would make an inspiring speech that would spark loyalty and bravery in his team. It was the sort of thing he'd read about in history books and it always seemed to work. After all, he was a top scholar and winner of the Most Sensible Boy in School for three years running. Jack pulled out a chair and stood on it. It wasn't something he would normally do, especially not in shoes, but it seemed appropriate in the circumstances.

'Listen to me,' he said, sounding braver than he felt. 'We may be thinkers, but today we must be greater than that. Today we must be WARRIORS, a TEAM fighting together against bullies and thugs, fighting together against fear and oppression. The PEN is mightier than the SWORD! WE are here in the name of our beloved school and we will never surrender! ST IMMACULATE'S FOREVER!' He grabbed Mr Snuggles from Fenella and thrust him into the air in a triumphant gesture. 'NEVER SURRENDER! FRIENDS, WHO'S WITH ME?

His team shuffled their feet and looked down at the floor. No one was with him. It was painfully clear to Jack that, once again, he was all on his own.

18

The Wings of War

The hall was a sea of colour, heaving with cheering pupils waving scarves and flags. They stood in their seats and clapped for all they were worth. The atmosphere crackled with excitement.

'Welcome to the final of the twenty-fifth Interschool End of Term Quiz Championship,' cried the quizmaster, striding on to the stage to a roar of applause. 'To my right I have the team from Brutus Academy of Saints & Heroes.' The Brutus team grunted and bumped fists. 'And to my right, I have the reigning champions: St Immaculate's School for the Gifted.' An ecstatic cheer went up from the audience while Jack's team stared miserably at their buzzers.

'Right,' said the quizmaster, shuffling his cards. 'Good luck, everyone. Here is the first question: What is the capital city of Hungary?'

Jack knew the answer; *everyone* in his team knew the answer – but they sat on their hands. At least Brutus wouldn't get any points if they didn't know the answers.

'Come on, this is an easy one. Anyone? The capital of Hungary?' The quizmaster looked disappointed. Rupert Pinspike was busy fiddling with something in his ear.

'I don't believe it!' whispered Jack to Aamir. 'Did you see that? He's wearing an earpiece – someone must be feeding them answers from the audience!'

'Er . . . Budapest?'

'Correct! Point to Brutus.'

Jack felt infuriated by the injustice; all the bullying was one thing but this blatant cheating was too much. He raised his hand to protest but Aamir yanked it back down. He gave him a hard stare and hissed, 'I'd like to get out of here alive.'

'Yes, leave it, Jack,' whispered Angus. They sat stock still – a row of frightened rabbits.

Headmistress Silk and Professor Bright exchanged looks of concern and disappointment.

Brutus quickly racked up an impressive score while the St Immaculate's team's total remained stubbornly at zero. 'All that *work*, all those *rehearsals*,' thought Jack in desperation, 'it was all a waste and now I'll be expelled for sure.' He sank his head on to the desk: the dream was over.

The quizmaster forged ahead:

'Please complete the last collective noun. "A pomposity of professors, a business of ferrets, a murder of . . ."?'

Pinspike from Brutus fiddled with his ear and slammed his hand on the buzzer. 'Crows, it's crows!'

'Correct! What is the sixth planet from the sun in the solar system?'

'Cawwww.' A raw and ragged croak came out of Pinspike's mouth.

The quizmaster looked up from his card. 'I beg your pardon?'

Pinspike swallowed, cleared his throat and tried again. 'Cawww!' He clamped his hand over his mouth in horror.

Jack lifted his head in surprise and stared. Had Pinspike just made the sound of a *crow?*

'Incorrect answer,' said the quizmaster. 'Lose one point. The answer is Saturn. In what year was the Victoria Cross medal first awarded?'

Furious, Pinspike slammed his hand down on the buzzer: 'CAWW!'

Everybody in the auditorium thought it was

a joke and broke into laughter. Everyone, that is, except for Jack. His heart rose up – Jack only knew one person that could make a boy sound like a crow. He sniffed – the faintest whiff of woodland hung on the air. Hardly daring to hope, his gaze swept around the auditorium.

Pinspike's teammates had wanted to snigger, but instead discovered they could only make the sounds of birds. Clucks, hoots, cheeps and twitters tumbled from their mouths. One of them began to peck at the desk and another began to flap his arms. Barry hopped up on to the desk and began to squawk 'CHEAT-CHEAT-CHEAT!'

Jack stood up in his seat, craning his neck to see. *Is she really here?* he thought, shielding his eyes from the glare of the spotlights. *Even after I tried to keep her away, has she really come to save me after all?*

And then he spotted her, perched on the back row of seats, grubby, tatty and ROARING with laughter. Jack wanted to jump up and down with sheer happiness! He had never been more pleased to see anyone in his life.

But there was no time to lose. Now the cavalry

had arrived, Jack knew he had to pull them back from the brink of disaster. He looked at the scoreboard and then at the big clock on the wall. Jack did a quick calculation and realised it was going to be a race against time; there were only minutes to go. Luckily he wasn't the sort of boy who wasted second chances.

He began to return answers like a turbo-charged tennis ace. 'What is the capital of Iceland?' 'Reykjavik.' WHACK! 'What is the correct way to address a Duke?' 'Your Grace.' WHACK! 'What does the K in JK Rowling's name stand for?' 'Kathleen.' WHACK! It wasn't long before they began to catch up with the hobbled Brutus team. Seeing that they were in trouble, one by one Aamir, Angus, Astrid and Fenella gradually began to join in. 'Molecules!' 'Nelson!' 'Gastric juice!' '1066!' Within five minutes the scoreboard was almost equal with the Brutus Academy on 108 and St Immaculate's on 107.

Full of fury, Pinspike snatched a pen out of Barry's fist. He began to scrawl the answers down and thrust them in the face of the quizmaster. 'CAWW!' he cried in triumph, his eyes crazed, 'CAWW!'

The crow hex used on the Brutus team should have been enough but Jack knew that Picklewitch was just getting going. She didn't know when to stop – and for once he was glad. With everyone focused on the unfolding comedy on the stage, Jack watched Picklewitch scrawl a muddy spell on the back windows, using all ten fingers and thumbs at the same time.

Rooks and ravens
Jays and wrens

Sparrows, starlings
Be my friends.

She hoicked up her dungarees and clambered on
to the windowsill. Her hands became a blur as she
wrote faster and faster, swirls and strange shapes
and symbols pulsing through the mud.

Claw, beak, mighty feather
Blackbirds, buzzards: flock together
Slow, then fast
then supersonic
Make my magic
MEGATRONIC!

A sharp draught sprinted around the room,
carrying with it familiar scents: mists and moss,
frost and smoke, earth and ash. Time's pendulum

stopped swinging for a brief moment and Jack became aware of a thrum of beating wings getting closer, louder and louder. It was like the noise he had heard that fateful day in the cemetery behind the school, only now it sounded like the pounding war drums of an advancing army. Something big was on its way.

All at once Picklewitch flung open the muddy windows and, like feathered hand grenades, hundreds of birds hurtled through. The spell had summoned them from the telegraph poles and the hedges, from parks and gardens, called them from the dark tangled woods and car parks and school sports fields, from the hills and farms. They poured through in a torrent, as if someone had pulled the plug out in the centre of the auditorium and all the birds in England were being sucked down a drain.

Gangs of squabbling sparrows mobbed the Brutus team. Sharp-beaked starlings pecked at their hair while woodpeckers hopped up their trouser legs and stabbed at their kneecaps. Bossy yellow-eyed seagulls stomped all over their desk and magpies stole all of their shiny blazer buttons, pens and badges. It was really very funny and the audience erupted into gales of laughter.

Then, just when the Brutus team thought they could take no more, it was the swallows' turn to shine, swooping in at top speed, bursting through. Fighter pilots in formation, they fired poo – *rat-a-tat-tat* – all over their smart navy-blue blazers. The final straw was when a family of owls landed on their desk and stared relentlessly at Barry until he cried.

Jack looked up at the clock – there

were only ten seconds left! The quizmaster battled valiantly on while the crowd chanted 'IM-ACC-U-LATE'S! IM-ACC-U-LATE'S!' They stomped their feet until the whole building shook. Headmistress Silk was standing on her chair and wolf-whistling. The teams were still neck and neck and St Immaculate's only needed to get one more question right to win. Jack had everything crossed that it was a question they could answer. '*Please* let it be on fossils, or weather patterns or the twenty-two times table.'

'So, now to the final question. What ...' bellowed the quizmaster, shielding his head from the sharp claws of robin, 'is the term for a witch's book of magic?'

Jack stood up and slammed his hand down on the buzzer so hard that he broke it. 'GRIMOIRE!' he laughed, in disbelief. 'It's a grimoire!'

'CORRECT!' The mighty gong clanged and the crowd erupted in thunderous applause.

19

St Immaculate's Forever

The birds vanished as quickly as they had appeared, as if sucked back up into the clouds by a heavenly vacuum cleaner. The cheering audience flooded the stage, clambering over seats, coats and bags in their excitement. Suddenly Jack was lifted off his feet and found himself carried aloft on dozens of hands. Even with a microphone the quizmaster had to shout to be heard over the roar of the crowd. 'Ladies and gentlemen, I give you the winners of the twenty-fifth Interschool End of Term Quiz, the reigning champions – *ST IMMACULATE'S SCHOOL FOR THE GIFTED!*'

Beaming and giddy with glory, Mrs Silk strode out of the wings, carrying the winner's cup. She handed it to Jack with a wink and, in this perfect golden moment, Jack knew that his place at St Immaculate's was safe. He held the cup above his

head in triumph, looking around for Picklewitch, but in all the kerfuffle he'd lost sight of her. He shouted over the racket: 'Picklewitch, where are you? Picklewitch!' But she was nowhere to be seen.

Later in the minibus, after they'd sung all the champion-themed songs they could think of, the children settled down into tired, happy chatter. Victoria got out of her seat and worked her way down the aisle to the front of the bus. 'Excuse me, Mrs Silk,' she said, her lips pursed, 'I'm afraid I have to report something very serious.'

Mrs Silk sat up straight and straightened her spectacles. 'Yes Victoria?'

Victoria glanced slyly back at Jack, the corner of her lip curled, and his soaring heart suddenly plunged. What was she going to say?

Victoria arranged her face into that of a pained saint. 'I'm afraid to tell you, Mrs Silk, that

Picklewitch is responsible for our victory, *not* Jack or the team. We won by cheating.'

Mrs Silk frowned. 'What on earth are you talking about, Victoria?' She looked over her shoulder at the rows of seats. 'Picklewitch isn't even on the bus.'

'Well,' said Victoria, 'I know that, but somehow – and I'm not sure how – she was in the auditorium. *She* was the one that made all those birds fly in and attack the Brutus team. It's not usual for flocks of birds to suddenly appear inside, is it? And you must have noticed the strange smell. I think I saw her ...' she lowered her voice to a whisper, '*casting spells!*' She held up her notebook: 'Look, I've been documenting the evidence for a while.' Victoria's eyes looked rather crazed and shiny. Jack wished his legs were ten feet longer so that he could kick her hard in the shins.

Mrs Silk coughed politely, her hand disguising a smile. 'Dear girl,' she said, 'I know Picklewitch has an eccentric way of dressing but are you saying that you think that she is an *actual* twenty-first-century witch?'

'Yes,' nodded Victoria, folding her arms. 'She is. I've even got a confession letter to prove it.'

The minibus radio, which, up until that moment, had been playing classical music, suddenly became much louder. Instead of Mozart, a newsreader's voice rang out.

'We are interrupting this broadcast to inform you that many incidents of odd bird behaviour have been reported in the area. Our expert says that it is a result of the east wind, 'cos everyone knows that's what makes birds all giddy-widdershins and behave like silly fopdoodles. Anyway, there's nothing to get your knickers in a twist about. As you were,

bamboozle-bamboozle-cough-cough.'

There was a crackle of static and the music faded back in.

Mrs Silk lowered her glasses and looked very sternly at Victoria. 'Well, there you are: a perfectly rational explanation. Now please sit down and kindly remember that there is no such thing as a real witch. I really expected more of a gifted girl like you, Victoria. St Immaculate's is not a school for the woolly-minded.' Only Jack noticed the ladybird on Mrs Silk's shoulder, flexing its wings before flying away home through a gap in the window.

Victoria did the walk of shame back to her seat while everyone stared and whispered, her cheeks burning red. As she passed Jack's seat he muttered, 'Tut. What a fudgenut.'

When the minibus finally pulled back into the

school car park, Jack stood up, turned around in his seat and held up his phone. 'Listen everyone, I have an announcement to make. I've just had a message from my mum to say that she has baked us all a special celebration cake and that it's in the assembly hall. It's huge – high as my head and big enough for everyone to have a piece!' An enormous cheer went up and Jack knew, his heart bursting with pride, that finally he was the most popular boy in the school. But he also knew that none of it would have been possible without the help of his very best friend: Picklewitch. Life would never be dull with her around. If only she were there to celebrate the victory with him – that would be the *real* icing on the cake.

As soon as the minibus doors opened there was a mad dash for the hall. *I'll have to make sure I save a big slice for Picklewitch*, thought Jack, clutching the silver cup under his arm. As he leant on the swinging double doors into the assembly hall, a thought occurred to him. *How odd that she's not here; it's not like her to miss out on cake.* But if Picklewitch had taught him anything it was that you should never judge a book by its cover . . .

Epilogue:

Just Desserts

Picklewitch wobbled the wheelbarrow down the street, huffing and puffing. She heaved it through the gate and down the bumpy path into the garden. It really was quite tiring, because cake was a lot heavier than it looked, especially a whole one that had so many silver balls and chocolate sprinkles on it.

As the birds dutifully stored the cake away in the branches of her walnut tree, crumb by crumb, Picklewitch gave a contented sigh. Jack was such a lucky boy and he had learnt so much about what it meant to be a good friend. She might even save him a slice.

Picklewitch nibbled at a fistful of cake and idly wondered if *she* had learnt anything. She polished her binoculars on her grubby dungarees and gave a little smile. Of course she hadn't, because Picklewitch knew everything already.

THE END

(For now)

DICTIONARY OF WURDS

Boxie — House dwellers

Elflocked — Perfect hairstyle (mayhaps knotty, with occasional burd nesting in it)

Fandanglery — See Trumpery

Flatterator — Iron

Fleabag – Cat

Flugelhorn — A wind instrument that witches cannot play

Glim-light — Candle

Grimoire — My book of secrets. PRYVIT. KEEP OUT. OR ELSE

Happy Hotbox — Oven

Hornswangler — A bad-tempered sheep sprite from Norway

Mugswoggler – An ill wind that makes tea go cold

Pannikin – Saucepan

Picklewitch – Master of Old Magic, Megatronic mostly, middling rarely. Best friend ever

Spy – Cat

Snitch – Cat

Trubblemaker – Cat

Trumpery – Fussy, frilly nonsense liked by Boxies. See Fandanglery

Whizz-cracking – Most excellent

YE OLDE INSULTS PIK N' MIX

Picaroon

Piepowder

Raggabash

Grubbler

Babbler

Mooncalf

Dozypox

Fudge-frazzler

Fudgenut

Hobbledehoy

Fopdoodle

Shollygaster

Stampcrab

Potzblitz driggle-draggle

Lubberwort

Mumblecrust

SPELLS

Spell to Summon a Storm Beest
Jangle the cobwebs
Kick sticks from the floor
Waft smoke with a feather
To make the wind roar.
Skywest and crooked
Now wind from the East
Add fire, earth and water
To call the Stormbeest.

Spell to Stop Tree Balding
Pickle a nut
Tickle a stone
Stroke a magpie
Go out alone.
Six for silver,
Seven for gold
Never be bald,
Chilly or cold.

Crow Hex

One Bloodroot, two Violet,
Moon waxing low,
Three Wolfsbane, four Wormwood,
Count all in a row.

Five Tangleweed, six Tansy,
North Wind he does blow,
Make the black-hearted frazzlers
Cackle like a crow.

BIRTHDAY WISH LIST

1. Sea foam
2. Rabbit's egg (blue)
3. Binocular polish
4. Tin of Ladymum's raspberry slices

SWEARS AND CURSES

Bat's bums
Weasel's Knickers
Fudgenuts
Spadger's Knees

PICKLEWITCH'S BEST AND MOST HILARIOUS JOKES

Q: What's brilliant and bounces?
A: A witch on a pogo stick.

Q: Why did the bad witch have to leave school?
A: She was ex-spelled.

Q: How do witches turn the lights on?
A: With a light's witch.

Q: What room has no floor, no window and no door?
A: A mushroom.

Q: What looks like half a walnut tree?
A: The other half.

Q: What's a tree's favourite shape?
A: A treeangle.

HOW TO MAKE WALNUT INK

- Gather 25 black, rotten old walnut husks (not shells).
- Put in pannikin. Add teacup of vinegar and cover in water.
- Bring to the boil and bubble gently for 20 mins.
- Cool and strain. Careful 'cos is proper messy.
- Use it to write very important and beautiful things with crow feather.

FACTS

Q: How many burds will fit in a bin lid?
A: 20 crows
   or 10 ravens
   or 105 robins
   (or 125 assorted tiny burds. Approx.)